BAD Mermaids

Meet the Sushi Sisters

SIBÉAL POUNDER

Illustrated by
Jason Cockcroft

BLOOMSBURY
CHILDREN'S BOOKS

LONDON   OXFORD   NEW YORK   NEW DELHI   SYDNEY

BLOOMSBURY CHILDREN'S BOOKS
Bloomsbury Publishing Plc
50 Bedford Square, London WC1B 3DP, UK

BLOOMSBURY, BLOOMSBURY CHILDREN'S BOOKS
and the Diana logo are trademarks of Bloomsbury Publishing Plc

First published in Great Britain in 2020 by Bloomsbury Publishing Plc

A catalogue record for this book is available from the British Library

ISBN: PB: 978-1-5266-1688-3; eBook: 978-1-5266-1687-6

4 6 8 10 9 7 5

Typeset by RefineCatch Limited, Bungay, Suffolk
Printed and bound in Great Britain by CPI Group (UK) Ltd, Croydon CR0 4YY

MIX
Paper from
responsible sources
FSC® C020471

To find out more about our authors and books visit www.bloomsbury.com
and sign up for our newsletters

For Jane and Edwin

BELUGA
TOWN

SALMON CITY

North America

OCTOPOLLI

PINKLY LAGOON

THE HIDDEN LAGOON

Pacific Ocean

South America

Atlantic Ocean

N

W E

S

The Mermaid WORLD MAP

Arctic Ocean

Europe

Asia

AMBERBERG

HERMIT GROVE

THE KINGDOM OF MUME

JEWELPORT

FORTRESS BAY

rica

RAINBOW LANDING

THE CROCODILE
KINGDOM

Australia

Indian Ocean

FROSTOPIA

Antarctica

Merry
Mary

Anchor
Rock

Swirly shell

Lobstertown

Clawacana
stadium

Crystal
Tunnel

Periwinkle
Palace

Oysterdale

The Hidden Lagoon

The Kelp Forest

Crabbyshell Highway

Hammerhead Heights

1

Paris Is Leaving

Paris pulled up her trademark knee-high socks and sighed as she leaned against a giant tank of pufferfish on the airport runway.

'I don't think it's coming,' she said to her mother, as they watched the planes roll past.

Their plane – the one with a giant sock logo on its tail – was nowhere to be seen.

'And shouldn't you change the sock design, now that you no longer make socks?' Paris said.

It was a good point. The Silkensocks family had made socks for generations, but now Susan Silkensocks, Paris's mother, had given up and started selling *mermaid* make-up to humans instead.

That's where the tank of pufferfish came in.

They were promotional fish for the make-up brand

Flubiére. The problem was, no human would buy make-up modelled on a fish, and so Paris's mother decided the whole family had to move to a place that would. And that place, she decided, was Scotland.

'We could stay here,' Paris said. 'I like California. It's going to be cold in Scotland.'

'Scotland is famous for its *fish*,' her mother scoffed. 'It's full of people who go there just for the fish. And I have a plan. I'm going to put all my promotional pufferfish in the loch next to our new home. That way, when people are fishing, they'll catch pufferfish covered in make-up and then they'll think, "Ah, I want some of that make-up." And that, Paris, is how I'll sell a lot of it.'

'That sounds … um,' Paris said slowly. 'I'm not sure people will want make-up that they've fished out of a loch.'

'After seeing these beauties, how could they *not*?' her mother said, pointing at the tank. A particularly large pufferfish was sliding its maroon-lipsticked mouth across the glass, making an unsightly smudge.

'Well, if we must go, we should get another plane,' Paris said. 'Clearly ours isn't coming.' She pointed at a bunch of people filing on to one nearby.

'We're not *sharing* a plane, Paris!'

'But most people do,' Paris said.

'Most people are idiots,' her mother snapped. 'If you have to share anything, you're doing it wrong.'

'That's not true,' Paris whispered to the pufferfish.

Just then, a tiny jet with a sock logo on it came

3

gliding in to land, then screeched to a halt in front of them.

The pilot clambered out.

'Sorry I'm late,' she said. 'It's Scotland, is it?'

'Unfortunately,' Paris said, flashing the pilot a smile.

'LATE!' Susan Silkensocks roared. 'My pufferfish could've crinkled, and most of them have smudged their lipstick!'

The pilot looked to Paris for answers.

'It's mermaid make-up,' Paris said. 'Modelled on pufferfish. Long story.'

'*Mermaid* make-up?' the pilot mouthed to herself in awe.

Paris climbed on board and sat on a plush sofa by the window. She pulled out her clamshell compact – the device she used to chat to her mermaid friends – and looked at it longingly. You see, Paris had a secret. She had once saved the Queen of the Mermaids from captivity, and as a reward she was given a magic necklace. When she shook it, she could morph into all sorts of things – a shark, a dolphin, a jellyfish, even a

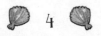

4

mermaid. That was how she came to have mermaid friends. She was itching to get to her new house so she could call them.

As soon as the pufferfish were secured, they took off. Paris sighed as she stared down at the ocean far below them – and the spot where her mermaid friends lived. Soon they'd be far away.

'Oh cheer up, Paris. We're going to live in a castle!' her mother oozed. 'A real *castle*. Once home to knights and a queen, and all the other bits that go in a castle. Swords and stuff.'

'It sounds freezing.'

'It's grand, Paris. GRAND. And then there's the loch. An ancient patch of deep, dark water that's supposed to be haunted by a mermaid!'

Paris looked up hopefully. A ghost mermaid sounded interesting.

2

Meri's Mysterious Mission

Meri Pebble, the spy mermaid, excelled at everything but patience.

'I want to do the most dangerous mission and I want to do it now!' she demanded. 'Send me anywhere, as long as it's the most impressively perilous, terrifying mission out there!'

Sabrina, the seahorse tasked with training the mermaids of Fortress Bay Spy School, inched her way up the canteen queue, trying to avoid her.

'Please, Sabrina? PLEASE? I've never been sent on an official mission and I'm ready. I really am.'

'Meri, have you ever considered calming down?' Sabrina said, as she spooned some sand on to a plate of crab cream with her tail. 'Or reining it in *just a tad*?'

'No, because I'm the best spy mermaid you have. I

saved the world,' Meri said. 'I'm practically a superhero. I helped unfreeze Realm Reach, and now mermaids can transport themselves to different lagoons and cities all around the globe. I *changed* the Mermaid World for the better.'

'Would you like a trophy? A parade in your honour? Maybe a city named after you?' Sabrina joked.

Meri looked off into the distance with misty eyes. 'Oh, that would be something.'

'Well, forget it,' Sabrina said, flicking some crab cream at her. 'You have your first World Wardrobe lesson this afternoon.'

'I already know what mermaids around the world wear, I don't need to go to World Wardrobe lessons.'

'Fashions change all the time,' Sabrina said. 'Just today, the mermaids of the Crocodile Kingdom started wearing shell-buckle belts again. It's important to know how to blend in when you're on a secret mission.'

Meri grabbed a Jellywich and furiously chewed on it. 'You know I'm the best, Sabrina. Give me a mission – *please*? PLEASE?'

Sabrina rolled her eyes. 'Well, I see it's either give you a mission or never eat lunch in peace again.'

Meri tried desperately not to grin.

'All the mission positions are currently filled, so don't look so happy,' Sabrina said. 'But I might have *something* that requires further investigation.'

'Something dangerous?' Meri asked hopefully, pulling out her clamshell compact. The spy compacts were used to communicate the details of each mission, and Meri was itching to find out what terrifying adventure awaited her.

'It's off-grid,' Sabrina said quietly, making Meri's tail jiggle with excitement. 'I received an anonymous tip and I'd like you to look into it. It involves humans and their safety.'

Meri thought of her friend Paris. She wasn't going to let anything happen to Paris.

'Here.' Sabrina slipped Meri a crabagram. 'Read this.'

'But,' Meri said, after she'd finished, 'it says THE SUSHI SISTERS ARE GOING TO DESTROY ALL THE HUMANS.'

'Shhh, keep your voice down,' Sabrina urged. 'It's highly confidential. We can't have our kind *hurting* humans.'

Meri burst out laughing. 'You do know who the Sushi Sisters are, don't you? They're *celebrities*. They make prank videos, and a lot of mermaids think they're really cool. They sell T-shirts and novelty hairbands with their faces on them. This is a joke, Sabrina! Someone's messing with you.'

'I didn't say it was true, did I?' Sabrina said. 'Say it *is* nonsense, the question then becomes – who would send such a thing?'

Meri stopped chewing her Jellywich and wiped her mouth. 'So you want me to find evidence that this is nothing but a joke?'

'Exactly,' Sabrina said.

Meri threw her arms in the air. 'That's hardly dangerous! What a waste of your *best* spy, Sabrina.'

Sabrina thrust some seaweed notes into Meri's hand. 'In terms of background, this should cover everything. The Sushi Sisters rose to fame when they

 9

competed on *Catwalk Prawn.*'

Catwalk Prawn was a TV show where mermaids competed to create the best tiny outfits for prawns.

'I know,' Meri said. 'My friends Beattie, Mimi and Zelda told me about it. When the Sushi Sisters were contestants, they—'

'Controversially shaved off the moustache of one of the judges as a joke,' Sabrina finished for her. 'And so they got kicked off the show and became *infamous*,' Sabrina continued. 'They got a TV show of their own called *Sushi Sisters' Prankathon*. And now, according to whoever wrote this crabagram, they're going to destroy all the humans.'

Meri laughed. 'It's nonsense, but fine, I'll happily prove the Sushi Sisters are nothing but famous and seriously spoilt mermaids. I'll follow them in one of the fancy Fortress Bay clam cars. A sea trip! Lady Wriggles is going to love it.'

Lady Wriggles was Meri's jellyfish assistant.

'I have a quick mission-related question before I go,' Meri said. 'What's sushi?'

'It's a type of food, popular in the human world,' Sabrina informed her. 'I personally don't trust any food created by humans, ever since I heard about toast.'

'Right,' Meri said. 'Well, I'll get started.' She turned to swim off, but Sabrina called after her.

'I think you've misunderstood!'

Meri turned round to see Sabrina holding a Sushi Sisters T-shirt.

'It just so happens that they've fired their assistant and need a new one. I'm sending you undercover. No fancy spy car, no sneaking around. And no Lady Wriggles.'

'But—'

'You'll be in full view,' Sabrina said. 'Working for them, looking after them—'

'You're saying I'm babysitting them!?' Meri cried.

Sabrina gave a hollow laugh. 'No, Meri, the Sushi Sisters aren't babies, and they're slightly older than you. Think of it as looking after a couple of badly behaved pets.'

Meri groaned.

 11

'I hear a rumble of excitement!' Sabrina teased. 'Your job is to gain their trust and figure out if there's any truth to this crabagram. And you will uncover the mermaid who sent it.'

'You're punishing me, aren't you?' Meri said. 'For boasting about saving the world.'

Sabrina chuckled. 'You'll be the assistant to two *famous and seriously spoilt mermaids*. I think that sounds almost fun.'

Meri sighed as Sabrina floated off to teach her next lesson.

'I'm not wearing the T-shirt!' she shouted.

Sometimes Meri *hated* being a spy mermaid.

3

Sleepover in the Hidden Lagoon

CLAMZINE

Today roving reporter Belinda Shelton has the pleasure of meeting the Sushi Sisters, the Hidden Lagoon's most popular mermaids!

Belinda joined the Sushi Sisters in their sushi-shaped submarine, nicknamed 'the fishvan'. Rumours about what's inside include a cartoon room for watching new cartoons before everyone else, and a special hatch for ordering any kind of food you want. Other more elaborate rumours include a collection of stolen moustaches and a miniature whale called Bob. Belinda was unable to verify any of these rumours as all the rooms in the fishvan were strictly off limits – aside from the plush sitting room, filled

 13

with Sushi Sisters merchandise, where this interview took place.

With only three episodes in their PRANKATHON series to go, the Sushi Sisters are taking to the sea, to play their pranks in three mystery locations. The first, we can exclusively reveal, will happen in H A M M E R H E A D HEIGHTS! Keep your eyes peeled and your tail swishes quick, or YOU might be the victim of their next prank!

BELINDA: *How far do you plan to travel to play your pranks? We know you have two locations left in the series after Hammerhead Heights.*

Should mermaids in Frostopia be on guard? Pinkly Lagoon? Octopolli?

THE SUSHI SISTERS: *We couldn't possibly tell – it would ruin the surprise. Let's just say, we plan to travel further than most mermaids have ever travelled before for our final prank of the season.*

BELINDA: *Try me – I've swum in every sea and seen almost all the sights.*

THE SUSHI SISTERS:
Even you haven't seen this place. It's a secret.

BELINDA: *Mysterious! And this final prank – any clues as to what it will involve?*

THE SUSHI SISTERS: *Us.*

BELINDA: *And ...*

THE SUSHI SISTERS: *Sushi.*

BELINDA: *Aaaand ...*

THE SUSHI SISTERS: *Something the world has never seen before.*

BELINDA: *WHAT IS THAT SWIMMING OVER THERE?*

[A note from the editor: Before entering the fishvan, Belinda Shelton signed a contract banning her from mentioning anything she might see in the fishvan that could ruin potential future pranks. For the record, we would like to state here that Belinda Shelton saw nothing strange in the fishvan. Absolutely nothing.]

Catch the Sushi Sisters on your shell screens tonight, or head on down to Hammerhead Heights to watch the prank unfold LIVE.

15

Beattie threw down the magazine. 'I need to watch the *Sushi Sisters' Prankathon* show! I can't miss it! Let's go to Hammerhead Heights! Is it almost night-time?'

Zelda stared at her.

'It's the morning, Beattie. You just woke up. You still have dribble on your chin and an eye mask half on your face.'

'Oh,' Beattie said. 'Well, I can't miss it later, all right?'

Zelda rolled her eyes. 'I don't know why you like the Sushi Sisters. I think they're mean – Wigbert Krill had been growing that moustache since *birth*.'

'He can grow another one,' Beattie protested.

'It won't be the same!' Zelda cried. 'It'll be a *completely* different moustache.'

'And they have cool outfits,' Beattie said.

'Beattie, they wear sushi. Sushi T-shirts, sushi shoulder pads, sushi earrings, sushi hairbands, sushi belts, sushi bangles, sushi *sunglasses*—'

'They like a theme,' Beattie interrupted. 'And apparently their fishvan is the coolest thing you've ever seen.'

'It's not,' Zelda said. 'It's a giant bit of fake floating sushi with windows.'

'Not the outside,' Beattie said, shaking her head, 'the inside! I've heard it's got a huge catwalk for testing outfits and a room with an unlimited supply of Sandcrackle cereal!'

'Listen to yourself!' Zelda cried. 'The Beattie I know would think testing outfits was ridiculous.'

'I think it's cool,' Beattie said.

'You think being well behaved and driving your clam car at a sensible speed is cool. The Sushi Sisters are a pair of maniacs tearing around the seas in a fishvan – they are everything that the Beattie I know *hates*.'

'Well, maybe I'm trying something new,' Beattie said with a pinch of anger in her voice. 'Maybe I'm bored of saving the world and being the one who always has to worry about everything. *Maybe* I want to relax and have fun, like the Sushi Sisters.'

Just then Mimi, Zelda's twin sister, floated into the room with three foam shakes.

'The Crab Café was completely sold out of Breakfast Foams, so I got their Foam Shake of the Day.'

'What *is* the flavour today?' Zelda asked suspiciously, knowing it was always a risky choice. Past flavours had included Seven-Hundred-Year-Old Seaweed, Human Garbage and Angry Crab Botóm.

'Jellyfish Zing,' Mimi said, just as Beattie took a sip and an electric current shot through her.

She turned to Mimi, her hair standing on end. 'Delicious!'

Mimi looked confused.

'Beattie would normally hate a drink that stung her,' she whispered to Zelda.

'This is the new Beattie,' Zelda said with a sigh. 'She's

decided she's going to be more like the Sushi Sisters than the friend we know and love.'

'Oh, I would love to meet the Sushi Sisters,' Mimi said. 'I heard they have a room in their fishvan that shows episodes of *Clippee* before anyone else has seen them.' Clippee the lobster was her favourite cartoon character.

'They don't,' Zelda protested. 'It's just a rumour, like all the other apparently cool stuff they have in there.'

She picked up the copy of *Clamzine* from the floor.

'Beattie, your mum interviewed them – what was the weird thing she saw in there? Look, at the end of the article she clearly sees something. What was it?'

Beattie stopped slurping her drink and looked around.

'I promised I wouldn't tell.'

'Yeah, but old Beattie wouldn't tell. New Beattie is more like the Sushi Sisters, and the Sushi Sisters *would* tell,' Zelda said, using the situation to her advantage.

'OK, well,' Beattie said, leaning closer. 'She saw something really strange peeking out at her from one of

the fishvan's many mysterious rooms.'

'I mean, we do live in the sea,' Zelda said. 'There's a lot of stuff peeking at us all the time.'

Beattie turned to see a family of fish staring at her from the window.

'They say "Bonjour",' Mimi said, translating for them because she was the only fishtalker in the group.

'What Mum saw wasn't something normal like a fish,' Beattie said. 'She said she'd never seen anything like it. She said it looked like a starfish, but it *had fur*.'

Zelda laughed. 'It's probably a starfish wearing Wigbert Krill's moustache. No one ever found it after the shaving, you know.'

'It wasn't a moustache,' Beattie insisted. 'It was alive. The Sushi Sisters are hiding something strange in there. Cods, they're so cool.'

'Did you just say Sushi Sisters?' came a familiar voice.

'Meri Pebble!' Zelda cried, swimming over to the window where the spy mermaid was floating. It had been a while since they'd seen her.

'Meri, you're just in time for a morning foam shake!' Mimi said brightly.

'Did you get the Jellyfish Zing flavour?' Meri asked.

'Wow, how did you know?' Mimi said. 'Is it because you're a spy?'

'No, I swam past the café on the way here and read the sign.' Meri turned to Beattie.

'Hey,' Beattie said casually, taking another sip of her electrifying foam shake.

'Beattie?' Meri said in surprise. 'There's something different about you.'

'It's her hair,' Mimi said. 'The foam shake makes it stand on end.'

'No,' Meri said. 'There's something else – I can't put my finger on it.'

'She's trying to act like the Sushi Sisters,' Zelda explained. 'It's her *new thing*.'

'About them,' Meri said. 'I have a favour to ask.'

'I'm not saving the world again,' Beattie said, raising her tail in front of her face in protest. 'It's taken its toll and now I'm going to be selfish and cool.'

'Oh no, this isn't about saving the world,' Meri said. 'I need help with a mission. I have to go on tour with the Sushi Sisters—'

Beattie choked.

'—and I was wondering if you'd come with me? Sabrina didn't say I *couldn't* have some extra help, so I thought we could all go undercover. I'll be their assistant and the rest of you can be their GLAM squad. You know, the people who make famous people look good – wardrobe, hair, make-up.'

The other mermaids stared at her.

'Oh please,' Meri said. 'Otherwise I'll have to go alone and it's going to be so boring.'

'YES!' Beattie roared, sending her foam shake flying. 'YES, YES, YES!'

'Not for me,' Zelda said flatly. 'And I don't think it's a good idea to let Beattie anywhere near the Sushi Sisters!'

Beattie had gone into a giddy trance.

'I mean, look at her,' Zelda said, before lowering her voice to a whisper. 'She's gone Sushi Sister crazy.'

'Sushi Sisters spelled backwards is sretsis ihsus!'

Beattie shouted excitedly.

'*See*,' Zelda said.

'Well, you haven't heard the reason I'm going undercover with them yet, Beattie,' Meri said.

Beattie shrugged. 'I'm cool with whatever it is. Count me in.'

'I like missions,' Mimi said with a kind smile. 'And if the Sushi Sisters have the special room with the *Clippee* cartoons then I might get to watch them early!'

'This is a terrible idea,' Zelda said. 'But I can't let you two go without me. Meri might be busy, and you need someone sensible to look out for you.'

'It won't be for long,' Meri said. 'I just need to figure a few things out.'

She read them the crabagram and told them about Sabrina's suspicions.

'I bet they *are* trying to destroy all the humans,' Zelda said. 'Look who you're fangirling about these days, Beattie!'

Beattie rolled her eyes. 'They would never do that. Someone is obviously pranking them by sending that crabagram.'

'But who?' Meri whispered.

'Probably Zelda,' Beattie said. 'Because she hates the Sushi Sisters.'

Meri looked sternly at Zelda, who held her hands in the air.

'I didn't send it,' she scoffed.

Meri flicked her tail. 'Well, we're going to find out who did.'

The pair of false teeth next to Beattie popped open and Steve, her talking pet seahorse, swam out. 'I'm coming too – I'd make an excellent fake make-up artist.'

Meri nodded in agreement. 'Oh, speaking of make-up – has anyone heard from Paris?'

'She's going to call as soon as she arrives in Scotland,' Beattie said.

'What if she loses her clam compact and can't reach us? Or what if she forgets about us completely?' Zelda said, sounding worried.

'It's not like you to worry,' Mimi said.

Zelda shot Beattie a look. 'It's not like Beattie *not* to worry.'

'So when do we meet the Sushi Sisters?' Beattie said, appearing beside Meri with a suitcase already packed.

'How did you get your suitcase?' Zelda said. 'You're in *our* bedroom.'

'She's magic,' Mimi reminded her.

Beattie was a water witch and she made magic and sold it in a catalogue with their friend Gronnyupple, who lived between the Crocodile Kingdom and Frostopia.

'You can't tell the Sushi Sisters you're magic,' Zelda said. 'They would definitely try to use you in their pranks. And they're dangerous enough without adding magic to the mix.'

'Chill out, Zelda, I won't,' Beattie said.

'And no using magic around them, even if you think they're not looking,' Zelda ordered. 'It's too risky. They can't know your secret.'

'Promise,' Beattie said, crossing her fingers behind her back.

4

The Ghost Mermaid

It was night-time when Paris arrived at Otterstone Castle.

Her new home.

The wind swirling over the loch sounded as though it was whispering to her. Paris couldn't shake the feeling that there was something below the surface.

'Could it be the ghost mermaid?' she whispered to herself.

Beattie and the others had told her there weren't any mermaids where she was going. The closest mermaid dwelling was Salmon City, but that was over a day's swim away.

'Paris, what are you doing?' her mother snapped as she struggled with the lock on the castle door.

'Nothing,' Paris said, staring up at the place, all dark

and empty. It was small for a castle, with four turrets and a tall wooden door surrounded by a strange stone carving of a monstrous eel. She edged closer to the loch, her shoes making the freezing gravel squeak beneath her feet.

'Well, do something useful!' her mother barked. 'Take the pufferfish to the water and let them stretch their legs.'

'They don't have legs, Mother.'

'You know what I mean!' her mother huffed. She turned her attention to her pufferfish. 'Don't swim too far, my beauties, our work begins tomorrow.'

So off Paris went, heaving the tank down to the loch. Despite the wind, the water was as smooth as glass.

'They say a ghost mermaid lives here,' Paris said to the fish. 'But I bet it doesn't. That would be too interesting.'

Just then she heard a giggle. It echoed around her and disappeared into the trees.

'Hello?' Paris whispered, suddenly not feeling so brave.

The giggle grew louder.

'I have no time for eerie ghosts!' she shouted. 'Enjoy your new home, pufferfish!' She hastily tipped the tank into the loch and ran back to the castle before the ripples on the water had time to vanish.

As she double-bolted the door and checked the locks were secure, a strange burning smell caught in her nose.

She whipped round to find her backpack was in the fireplace and very much on fire.

'My inventions are in there!' Paris cried. 'And my clam compact!'

'But there was nothing else to burn and I'm freezing,' her mother said, as Paris plunged a hand in to rescue it.

'Ouch!' she cried,

reeling back, clutching something.

'That's just a shell,' her mother said, unaware it was the only way Paris had of communicating with her mermaid friends. 'I'll get you another one.'

Paris stared down at the burned compact, her eyes filling with tears.

'Your hand!' her mother cried. 'You've burned it. Outside, quickly! The castle isn't connected to the water mains yet, so you'll have to dunk it in the loch.'

Paris's eyes grew wide.

'Well?' her mother said. 'What are you waiting for?'

Paris had intended never to return to the loch, and yet here she was again, a whole minute later.

She approached slowly and found a nice big boulder to sit on.

'I'M DIPPING MY HAND IN, CREEPY GHOSTS! NO FUNNY BUSINESS!' she roared.

The freezing loch made a hissing sound as her hand entered the water and steam billowed up into the trees.

'Aaaah,' she said with relief. It felt good on her burn and, so far, no ghost had tried to pull her under.

It wasn't until she set off back to the castle that she heard the giggle again.

Paris whipped round, but there was no one there – just water and rocks and the trickle of light from the castle. She narrowed her eyes and whispered, 'I am Paris Silkensocks, Gadget Queen and Part-Time Mermaid, and I mean no harm. Please stop the creepy giggling.'

As she took another step towards the castle, the water behind her splashed!

The giggle grew louder.

She slipped and fell to her knees. Without looking back, she crawled as fast as she could and collapsed in a breathless heap on the castle floor.

'You look like you've seen a ghost,' her mother said.

'I have!' Paris cried. 'Well, I heard one.'

Susan Silkensocks laughed.

'Don't be silly, Paris. People made up the ghost so they'd have something to talk about. But you wait – now

31

we've brought Flubiére to town, they'll soon forget the ghost!'

Paris got to her feet, clutching her necklace tightly. If there was a ghost in the loch, she was going to get to the bottom of it.

5

Meet the Sushi Sisters

The Sushi Sisters' floating fishvan rested on one of the huge rock towers that made up Hammerhead Heights.

It was a little van, and looked even more so next to Jawella's, the famous shark with a restaurant in its mouth. Mermaids queuing for tables were doing their best to ignore it. It was fair to say the mermaids of Hammerhead Heights were not huge fans of the Sushi Sisters.

Beattie steered the clam car towards the shark, her hands gripping the shell steering wheel so tightly it was cracking under her fingers.

'Why is the clam car making a *put-putting* noise?' Zelda said, staring out of the back window. Trails of black goo were coming from the exhaust.

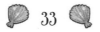 33

'It probably needs more eel juice,' Beattie said with a shrug.

'Clam cars need to be filled with eel juice?' Zelda cried.

'I didn't know that,' Mimi said airily.

'Yes, it needs eel juice,' Beattie said faintly. 'I always fill it up – have you never noticed? I *always* do the boring, sensible things, but NOT ANY MORE! I didn't bother checking before we set off this time, because who cares if the clam car breaks down?'

'I care!' Zelda shouted. 'What if we'd broken down on the Crabbyshell Highway? We could have been squashed by a sea lion!'

The clam car gave one final *put-put* and turned belly-up, sinking fast until it landed on the back of a disgruntled hammerhead shark.

'See?' Beattie said, as the shark bucked them off and sent them sailing straight on to a rock tower with a crunch. 'Everything is *fine*.'

'GET OFF MY TOWER!' an angry mermaid with a shark tail growled, pointing at a *NO PARKING* sign.

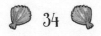

Beattie grabbed her suitcase and swam off.

'Beattie!' Zelda cried. 'We can't just leave the clam car wedged on a rock tower.'

'We can do anything!' Beattie called back. 'That's the beauty of not caring!'

Zelda growled and pushed the clam car off the roof of the rock tower, settling it in a parking spot nearby. 'I don't like it when Beattie is like this,' she said, pausing before she said the next bit. 'It means *I* have to be responsible.'

Steve floated up beside her. 'I *know*. Me too. I want old Beattie back.'

It was the first time Zelda and Steve had ever agreed on anything and they both felt weird about it.

Meri swam off to catch up with Beattie, who was eagerly floating by the fishvan door.

'Here goes nothing,' Meri said with a sigh as she knocked lightly.

'They might not hear that!' Beattie cried, hammering hard with both fists. When no one answered, she began whacking the door with her tail.

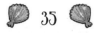 35

'HELLO, SUSHI SISTERS!' she screeched. 'GLAM SQUAD HERE!'

'Bet you wish you'd done this mission alone,' Zelda whispered to Meri, who was covering her eyes. 'And if you think about it, the mission hasn't really started yet. Just think how bad things could get …'

The door flew open and the Sushi Sisters emerged like eels from a cave. They wore little sushi earrings and huge hairbands dotted with sushi rolls. Their eye make-up was bright orange.

Beattie was shaking with excitement.

Meri cleared her throat and said, 'Hello, I'm Meri, your assistant for the tour, and this is the GLAM squad.'

'I'm Beattie – I do make-up,' Beattie said.

'She's my assistant,' Steve said, butting in. 'I'm Steve, talking seahorse and make-up legend – I only work with limited-edition Flubiére.' He had said *he* would like to do make-up, and he wasn't about to let Beattie take that away from him.

'Zelda – I do clothes,' Zelda said reluctantly. 'I'm a … waistcoat expert.'

'Mimi. And I do …' Mimi paused, having forgotten what to say.

'Hair,' Zelda finished for her.

Mimi bowed. 'I am HAIR.'

'We were expecting an assistant but not the GLAM squad,' the sister with the long orange hair said.

'That's Vetty,' Beattie whispered to Steve. 'She's my favourite.'

'I don't know if we need a GLAM squad,' Vetty said.

Meri gulped.

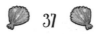

'We come with the assistant,' Zelda said, pushing her way to the front. 'Our boss … um … Mr Hairspray Tights, yes, Hairspray Tights, wanted you to have a GLAM squad, just in case. We're the best in the world.'

'Your boss is called Mr Hairspray Tights?' the sister with shorter hair said, sounding unconvinced.

'That's Nolla,' Beattie whispered excitedly to Steve. 'She's the other Sushi Sister.'

'Mr Hairspray Tights wanted a human name to make him stand out from the crowd,' Zelda said. 'Apparently, Hairspray Tights is a very common name in the human world.'

'We did a summer on land with legs and we never met anyone called Hairspray Tights,' Vetty said.

'You were probably … on the wrong … bit of land?' Zelda mumbled.

'Well, you'll have to sign this before you can work for us,' Vetty said, brandishing a roll of seaweed. 'Under no circumstances are you to talk about us to anyone. There's also a copy of the fishvan rules.'

Beattie unrolled the huge seaweed scroll.

'The key ones are – never speak to us unless spoken to,' Nolla said. 'No hugging unless a hug is requested. And no weird items, however small, so you can't take those false teeth inside.'

Steve gasped. 'It's not a pair of false teeth – it's MY BEDROOM!'

Vetty glared at him. 'I'm afraid the rules are set in seaweed.'

'Fine,' Steve said, as Beattie began strapping the false teeth to the roof of the fishvan.

'Oh, and no saying our special word unless given permission,' Nolla said.

Zelda rolled her eyes.

'They say "SUSH" when they say the same thing or wear matching outfits,' Beattie oozed.

'See, you just said it, and that would be an instant ban from the fishvan,' Vetty said.

Beattie's face fell.

'When you're in the van you can call us by our real names – Vetty and Nolla. But outside the van we're the Sushi Sisters. Got it?'

'IT'S THE SUSHI SISTERS!' came a cry, as a clump of mermaids swam towards them.

'Quick,' Vetty said. 'Get inside.'

Beattie couldn't believe it. The fishvan was a lot bigger than it appeared on the outside, and a lot cooler. They followed the Sushi Sisters through a comfy shell seating area, with sushi-shaped cushions and a little kitchen, then down a long corridor, past dozens of sushi-shaped doors.

'All out of bounds, apart from this one,' Vetty said, stopping at a sign that said *NOT OUT OF BOUNDS*.

She threw open the door to reveal a tiny bunkroom with four shell bunks.

'You'll sleep in here. We go to bed late and wake up early, so you won't get much sleep. I've left a seaweed folder with the itinerary over there.'

Meri plucked it from the bed and began rifling through it.

'It tells you everything you need to know, including

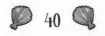

our favourite breakfast cereals, lipstick colours and clothes.'

'You pick the bunk you want first,' Vetty said to Meri, flashing her a smile. 'Because you are our *favourite*.'

'I am?' Meri said.

'You're so lucky,' Beattie oozed. 'I'd *love* to be their favourite.'

'We'll give you a few minutes to settle in,' Nolla said. And off they swam, down the corridor and into one of the restricted rooms.

Meri chucked the folder down and stared out at the shark-infested waters of Hammerhead Heights. 'I can't believe Sabrina gave me this mission.'

'It's a prison,' Zelda said, staring at the bunks. 'What now?'

Beattie swam in excited circles. 'Now we hang out with the Sushi Sisters and be seriously cool and pranky!'

'No,' Meri said with a glint in her eye. 'Now we find what we came here for.'

6

The GLAM Squad Gets to Work

While Beattie, Steve and Mimi were doing the Sushi Sisters' hair and make-up, Zelda and Meri took the opportunity to sneak around the fishvan looking for evidence.

'Let's check their bedroom first,' Meri said, inching the door open.

The Sushi Sisters' bedroom was not what they expected – there were shell beds and floating clothes being nibbled by fish, and just generally a lot of mess.

'I was expecting a secret lair,' Zelda said, sounding disappointed.

Meri began rifling through drawers and swimming under the beds. 'Help me look, Zelda,' she said. 'There could be something hidden away.'

Zelda caught a waistcoat floating past. 'The only

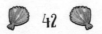

thing the Sushi Sisters are hiding in here is how *ordinary* they are. I don't like them, but I really doubt they're trying to destroy all the humans.'

'Zelda!' Meri hissed from under one of the beds. 'Get under here.'

Meri was floating on her back and looking up at something stuck to the underside of the bed.

Two pairs of shoes. *Human* shoes.

'What is this?' Zelda said.

'Exactly.' Meri grinned. 'Why do they have them?'

'Maybe they're for shockey ...' Zelda whispered, even though she knew it couldn't be true. Shockey, her favourite game, only required one human shoe, which was used as a shockey puck. There was no need for a pair. In fact, these shoes were so perfect, so brand new, no one would ever play shockey with them.

Meri shook her head. 'These shoes have been hidden. Why would a mermaid need secret shoes?'

'If they were planning to go on land,' Zelda said.

'Yes ...' Meri said.

'To destroy all the humans!' Zelda cried.

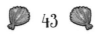 43

Meri wriggled with excitement.

'Not sure I'd do it in rainbow-coloured ballet flats though ...' Zelda mumbled.

'The crabagram is true!' Meri said. 'This *is* a dangerous mission. Oh thank cods for that!'

'*Meri*,' Zelda spluttered. 'You can't seriously be happy that the Sushi Sisters are planning to destroy all the humans. This is not good news.'

'No, you're right,' Meri agreed. 'It's BRILLIANT NEWS! Oh, I'm so excited it's a proper mission! Obviously, I'll never let them destroy the humans, so we don't need to worry.'

'Don't need to worry!?' Zelda cried, wriggling out from under the bed. 'Meri, we've got to warn Paris.'

Meri slipped out from under the bed too and began swimming in excited circles. 'Unnecessary. Don't worry, Zelda. To get legs they will need permission from Arabella Cod. And she will *never* give it to them – they're known for pranking, and they've already done their summer on land with legs. She won't let them loose up there again.'

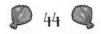

'So they must have another plan. Who else can give them legs?' Zelda asked.

'Well, spies can get approval for legs from Sabrina,' Meri said, whipping out her clamshell compact.

'And what if they ask Sabrina?' Zelda said.

Meri laughed. 'How would they contact her? She's a top-level spy! Only a select few Fortress Bay mermaids have a direct line to her! Including myself.'

Zelda eyed the clamshell compact.

'Ah,' Meri said. 'Good point. I'll keep my clam compact safe at all times.'

'So what do we do now?' Zelda asked.

'We need to keep this between us,' Meri said. 'The others will give the game away. No telling your sister, and definitely not Beattie.'

'No one but us,' Zelda said, giving Meri a fist bump.

'We'll watch them closely. They have the shoes, so they must be confident they can get legs,' Meri said. 'We can't let those Sushi Sisters out of our sight!'

A door banged and Meri and Zelda watched as the Sushi Sisters swam past the window and off

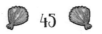

into the distance.

'And we've already failed,' Zelda said.

'Um,' Steve said, appearing in the doorway, covered in make-up. 'I'm not sure the Sushi Sisters believe we're hair and make-up professionals.'

'Why not?' Zelda asked.

'Well, I think the final straw was when Beattie put lipstick on their cheeks.'

7

Prank One, Hammerhead Heights!

Outside the fishvan fans of the Sushi Sisters were eagerly floating near the octopus camera crew. The stars were huddled at a safe distance, with Beattie and Mimi acting as their bodyguards.

'How come you get to hang out with the Sushi Sisters?' one young mermaid asked Beattie.

'Because I'm a really cool mermaid now,' Beattie said.

Mimi snort-laughed, but stopped when she realised Beattie was serious.

'I am,' Beattie said, glaring at her. 'I'm really cool, just like the Sushi Sisters.'

Behind them, Vetty and Nolla were discussing the prank in loud whispers, so Meri and Zelda edged closer to listen in.

'The delivery dolphins will soar overhead and dump

the foam shakes on Jawella's,' Vetty said.

Zelda gasped. 'You can't do that to the Jawella's shark. He's—' But Meri pulled her away before she could finish.

'Zelda, what are you doing?' Meri whispered. 'We can't argue with them about the prank – we have to let it play out. They need to think we're on their side, or we'll be flicked out of the fishvan before we can discover their plan.'

'But he's just a harmless old shark. They can't prank a shark, they're the most gentle, harmless things in the sea!'

Mimi swam over, sensing her twin was upset.

'Have you ever heard a shark say a bad word about anyone, Mimi?' Zelda asked.

'No, I haven't,' Mimi said. 'Sharks only ever have nice things to say.'

Zelda looked at Meri, her eyes wide and hopeful.

'I'm sorry, Zelda,' Meri said. 'We can't tamper with the prank. The Jawella's shark will understand. The Sushi Sisters have to trust us. As far as they're concerned, you two are experts in waistcoats and hair, and you're fully supportive of their pranks.'

'I AM HAIR,' Mimi said grandly.

'Oi!' Zelda yelled over to the Sushi Sisters before Meri could stop her. 'What flavour foam shakes did you choose?'

Vetty and Nolla glared at her.

'Jellyfish Zing,' Vetty said. 'But it's none of your business.'

Zelda scrunched up her fists. 'That might *hurt* him. Beattie looked like she'd been electrocuted when she drank it.'

'That's the whole point,' Vetty said with a shrug. 'The shark will go crazy and every mermaid dining inside will be spat out. And if any mermaid gets hurt, we can just blame the shark.'

'Ah, I see the Crab Café order heading this way,' Nolla said. 'Vetty, it's time to start the show – let's get in position.'

In the distance fifty dolphins wearing crabs on their heads were gliding towards them.

'Glowfish! Shell camera! Action!' came a cry and the Sushi Sisters began twirling in front of the cameras. Beattie watched in awe.

'It's time for another prank!' Vetty said. 'But before we get started, I want to tell you a little bit about my brand-new hairband made by Figgy Bass, and my really cool shell and squid ink earrings, featuring Clippee the cartoon lobster!'

'If the pranks are so funny, I don't know why the Sushi Sisters can't prank each other instead,' Zelda grumbled to Beattie. 'Jawella's is just a sweet shark floating about as a restaurant and minding his own business. They should pick on someone their own size.'

Beattie wasn't listening, and it was extremely pleasant – not having to worry or not trying to fix things was so easy.

'Zelda! Is that you?' came a shout. Riley Ramona, a shockey player for the Hammerhead Heavyweights, was making his way over to them, grinning a gappy grin. Zelda had once accidentally knocked out his front tooth by accident in a particularly gruelling match.

 50

'What are you doing in Hammerhead Heights, Zelda?' Riley asked. 'Aren't you meant to be at shockey camp with your teammates?'

Zelda gritted her teeth and looked from the Crab Café dolphins to the Sushi Sisters and back again, as if measuring the distance. 'I'm here to do a little prank,' she whispered, before shooting out of sight.

Meri spun round frantically on the spot. 'Where did Zelda go!?'

Mimi shrugged. 'I have a dizzy head. I normally get one when she's playing sports somewhere. I can always tell when she's swimming fast. So my guess is she's swimming fast somewhere.'

'She muttered something about a prank?' Riley said with a shrug. 'Are you a new mermaid? I don't think we've met?'

Meri pushed him aside and began frantically scanning the sea for Zelda.

'Beattie,' Meri said, swimming over and shaking her urgently. 'Did you see which way Zelda went?'

'Not a clue,' Beattie said.

'I think she might be trying to ruin the prank,' Meri said.

Beattie looked over to where the Crab Café dolphins were floating. 'But she can't do that.'

'Exactly,' Meri said. 'I don't want the Sushi Sisters to flick us out of the fishvan. Only one spy mermaid has ever failed her first proper mission, and do you know what her name was?'

'Nope,' Beattie said.

'Exactly!' Meri wailed. 'Because she got kicked out of spy school and never spied again.'

'To be fair,' Beattie said, 'no ordinary mermaid would know the name of any spy – because they're meant to be stealthy and, well, spies.'

'Not the point,' Meri said, spitting the words in frustration. 'We need to stop her.'

'We don't,' Beattie said. 'When I said "she can't do that", I meant she actually can't. Everyone knows the Crab Café dolphins only respond to the mermaid who placed the order. They won't listen to Zelda. She can try and stop them, but they'll only listen to the Sushi Sisters.'

Meri sighed with relief. Beattie was right – it was the most basic of Hidden Lagoon knowledge. The Crab Café dolphins only listened to the mermaid who placed the order – they had covered it in Mermaid Food and Foam Shakes class on more than one occasion.

'Craaaaaaab Caaaafféeeee deliverrrrrrrrryyyyy!' came the trill from a seriously excited Nolla.

As the dolphins soared overhead, smirks spread across Nolla and Vetty's faces.

'This should be interesting,' Zelda said, slipping in between Beattie and Meri.

'Zelda,' Meri said sternly. 'Where did you go? Why do you look so delighted with yourself? What have you done?'

Zelda crossed her arms and smugly stared up at the dolphins. 'Absolutely nothing. What makes you think I've done something?'

The dolphins stopped above Jawella's and in one swift move dropped the foam shakes on to the poor shark. The contents oozed out, covering it completely.

But instead of getting a shock, the Jawella's shark

started wiggling happily.

Nolla's face fell.

'The shark … loves it.'

'WHAT IS GOING ON?' Vetty screamed.

'Crab cream,' Zelda whispered to Meri, pointing to a large razor-clam delivery car. 'The driver was on her way to deliver it to the restaurant, so I did a little switcheroo and swapped it for the Jellyfish Zing shakes. The Jawella's shark LOVES crab cream. This is such a treat for him.'

The shark shook like a dog in mud, covering the Sushi Sisters from head to tail in crab cream.

'THE PRANK IS RUINED!' they screamed together. 'Sush.'

The crowd erupted into laughter and pointed at the Sushi Sisters.

'PRANK'S ON THEM!'

'THAT BACKFIRED!'

'HAHAHAHAHAHAHA!'

Zelda turned to Beattie – even though they too were coated in crab cream, Beattie could tell Zelda

was pleased with herself.

'Did you do this?' Beattie growled.

Zelda shook her head. 'I wish I could take credit for this excellent work. Whoever did this is a *genius*.'

'STOP THE CAMERAS!' Nolla wailed. 'STOP THE CAMERAS NOW!'

Vetty scrunched up her fists. 'Let's go to the fishvan and review the footage – I want to see who switched the foam shakes and RUINED our prank!'

'This,' Meri whispered to Zelda, 'is a BIG problem.'

8

The Furry Things in the Fishvan

Zelda wasn't worried.

'What if they see you on the footage?' Meri fretted. 'My mission will be ruined.'

'They won't,' Zelda assured her.

'Did you use a disguise? Or ask another mermaid to switch the contents of the cups? *Why* are you so confident they won't see you when they review the footage?'

'Because—' Zelda started, but the Sushi Sisters interrupted.

'Hurry up, slowmaids, the screening room is in here!' Nolla said.

Behind the out-of-bounds door sat a room filled with screens.

'It's my favourite lobster in a dress!' Mimi chirped,

pushing past the others and floating in front of a *Clippee* cartoon. 'And it's an episode I haven't seen before, but I've seen them all …'

'Yeah, this is a brand-new one,' Vetty said, as if it wasn't a big deal.

'Wow,' Meri whispered to Beattie. 'This is an impressive set-up.'

Vetty grabbed a rock remote control and switched all the screens to the Jawella's tape. There were various angles on display.

'Now we'll see who RUINED our prank,' Nolla said, hitting play.

'Where's Beattie?' Mimi asked.

Zelda shrugged.

'I think she was getting the crab cream out of Steve's snout.'

Outside, Beattie had been holding Steve by the tail while he blew his nose vigorously.

'That crab cream really got stuck,' he wailed as they

swam back to the fishvan.

The problem was, the others had already settled themselves inside – but where?

'The fishvan rooms are off limits unless we have permission.' Beattie rested her ear against the first door, hoping to hear something. When she didn't, she moved on to the next door, and then the one after that.

Steve rolled his eyes. 'They aren't going to know if we peeked in every room. We should just do it, Bea—'

She held a hand in the air to shush him.

'I hear something in here,' she whispered. 'Ripples in the water and clinking sounds.'

Steve swam over. 'I would've thought they'd be screaming by now, if they've seen the footage of what happened with the foam shakes.'

Beattie inched the door open and peered inside.

It wasn't the room Zelda, Meri, Mimi and the Sushi Sisters were in, but there was someone in there.

Or some*thing* …

9

Emergency Mode

Paris watched her mother tempt the pufferfish back into their tank with clumps of glitter. It was a well-known fact that the Flubiére fish would do anything for glitter. Flubiére fish were even *paid* in glitter. They stored it in their bellies, and that's why some of the make-up had glitter in it – because a Flubiére fish threw up on some lip gloss and a mermaid thought it actually looked pretty good. Or so Mimi said.

Paris picked up her burned clamshell compact and a screwdriver and began fiddling with the buttons. She'd always liked inventing gadgets, but since she'd been given the magic necklace, she hadn't made anything new – what was the point when you already owned the greatest invention in the world?

She was determined to fix the clamshell compact

though. It was the only way she could communicate with her mermaid friends, unless she swam. But from Scotland that would take days and days, and she'd never swum that far before. She wondered if she could secretly get a flight back to California and swim from there like she used to.

'Mother!' she called from the window. 'I might take a little holiday while you're busy selling Flubiére! I'm thinking a trip to California.'

'WE JUST CAME FROM THERE!' her mother snapped back. 'And no, Paris! We're having a grand party to introduce ourselves to the locals. I'm calling it a Flubiérarty, which is very catchy.'

Paris groaned.

'I'll need your help serving the canapés.'

Paris chucked the screwdriver across the room and sighed. 'I just want to speak to my friends,' she muttered, shaking the clamshell compact and punching the buttons at random.

The screen flickered. She leapt up!

'HELLO?' she shouted.

The screen crackled.

'THIS IS JELLY OF WHALE BUS FAME. I AM PICKING UP AN EMERGENCY CALL IN THE UPPER REALMS. MERMAID, PLEASE RESPOND.'

'JELLY!' Paris cried. She couldn't see the old mermaid on the screen, but she was relieved to hear her voice.

'Ah, Paris! How lovely to hear you, even if it is crackly. Do you need help? Please state your emergency.'

'I'm trying to get in touch with Beattie, Mimi and Zelda,' Paris said urgently. 'I've moved to Scotland and I need to speak to them, but I damaged my clam compact and it doesn't seem to be working properly. Can you transfer my call?'

'No can do, little mermaid,' Jelly said. 'You've broken your clam compact and it's on emergency mode – that means it will only communicate with me.'

'Oh,' Paris said quietly.

'But, GOOD NEWS,' Jelly said. 'I'm on my way to Salmon City to drop off some mermaids, so I could pick you up there and take you back to the Hidden Lagoon.'

Paris leaned out of the window and watched her

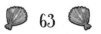

mother roll the tank of pufferfish down the drive.

'Thank you, Jelly, but I can't. I've got a Flubiérarty to attend and my mother would—' she stopped. A ghostly pale boy was peeking out of the loch.

She leaned further out of the window to get a better look.

He stared up at Paris and waved, making her stumble back into her room.

'Are you all right, Paris?' Jelly asked.

'Yes. Sorry,' Paris said. 'Thanks for the offer of help, but I have to go!'

She tore outside, clutching her magic necklace.

10

Hamstars

The Sushi Sisters reviewed the tapes of the failed prank, but it was no good.

'It's a mermaid blur,' Nolla said. 'We'll never know who did it.'

Zelda smiled smugly at Meri. No camera would be able to capture her when she was travelling at full speed.

'Aaargh!' came a scream from the hallway.

'Beattie!' Zelda, Mimi and Meri said at once.

They shot out of the screening room to find Beattie and Steve floating next to an open door.

'I didn't mean to open it!' Beattie cried.

'Oh great,' Vetty said flatly. 'Our secret is out.'

Zelda and the others floated on the spot, their mouths hanging open.

'Are you seeing what I'm seeing?' Zelda whispered to the others.

'Furry faces,' Mimi chirped. 'With starfish bodies.'

'Is that ... a hamster from land mixed with a starfish?' Meri asked.

Nolla shook her head. 'It's a ham*star* not a ham*ster*.'

'What's a hamster?! And what's a hamstar?!' Beattie cried.

'I thought you'd done a summer on land,' Meri said. 'A ham*ster* is a cute little rodent, and popular human pet.'

'How come you know so much about human pets?' Zelda whispered.

'We have mermaid spies who live in the human world,' Meri explained in a hushed voice. 'Joey Sharkton once visited our spy school and did a lecture on human pets. They keep dogs and cats and hamsters and sometimes parrots, which are a type of opinionated bird.'

'But this creature has a hamster face and a starfish body,' Beattie said. 'How did a land creature get mixed with a sea one?'

'Seriously, Beattie,' Zelda said. 'You've seen mercats and you're questioning that?'

'Why don't we ever question that?' Beattie said. 'I mean, it's *half cat, half fish.*'

Steve cleared his throat. 'Um, Beattie, you're *half human, half fish.*'

'Well, I know that,' Beattie said. 'But what I mean is, where do these half-and-half creatures come from? Where did *we* come from?'

'Are you *worrying* about where we come from?' Zelda asked hopefully.

'No, no, definitely not,' Beattie said, clearing her throat awkwardly. 'I don't worry about anything any more, remember?'

'Well,' Vetty said, scooping up the hamstars. 'Now that you've met our top-secret pets, you can

look after them too.'

'What are their names?' Mimi asked.

'Ham and Star,' Nolla said.

'Of course,' Zelda said, rolling her eyes.

'Steve, you can watch Ham, because you're *terrible* at make-up,' Nolla said.

Steve's eyes grew wide. 'Beattie was the one who put lipstick on your cheeks!'

Beattie shoved him in her hair before he could say anything that would get them thrown out of the fishvan.

'And, Mimi, you can look after Star,' Vetty said, 'because you are *terrible* at hair.'

Mimi scooped up the little hamstar and smiled. 'Oh, I could do its hair!'

'NO!' Vetty and Nolla shouted at once.

Nolla handed Mimi a top with huge goldfish-bowl shoulders. 'We were given this by Figgy Bass. You can borrow it and keep the hamstars safe on your shoulders. If anyone asks where you got them, say they're old toys and you're not telling.'

'No one else in the world owns a hamstar, and we

want to keep it that way,' Vetty said. 'It's *our* thing.'

'Where did you get them?' Beattie asked.

'A secret place,' Vetty said mysteriously.

'There's no such place,' Meri laughed.

'Of course there is,' Vetty said. 'Everyone knows there are secret waters, undiscovered places and hidden cities. You know, like the one mermaid spies live in.'

'Pah!' Meri said, desperately trying to be casual. 'Mermaid spies aren't real. I don't know where you heard that but mermaid spies are not a thing.'

'Everyone knows spies are real,' Nolla said. 'And everyone knows spies can do anything.'

'*Spies* rhymes with *lies*, which means they're not true,' Meri said, giggling nervously.

'So what's next?' Zelda said, changing the subject for Meri's sake. 'Where's your next prank?'

The Sushi Sisters smirked.

'All in good time, Zelda. First we have a very important shopping appointment with Figgy Bass at Sandbury's, and you're all coming with us.'

69

11

Shopping with the Sushi Sisters

Sandbury's department store sat in Swirlyshell's popular shopping district. It was a nine-storey shell-studded building bursting at the seams with everything from Flubiére make-up to human shoes and bathtubs.

It was a shop Beattie, Mimi, Zelda and Steve had visited many times, and Meri had watched mermaids swimming around outside it while practice-spying on their tails back in Fortress Bay.

'Oh, I can't wait to finally ride in the dolphin carriages!' Meri said, flopping into one.

Sandbury's was famous for its dolphin assistants, who would pull you in their sleighs to any section of the shop you desired.

'Fashion on the Secret Top Floor,' Vetty said. 'We have a private appointment with Figgy Bass.'

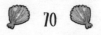

'Then you'll need the VIP dolphin assistants,' a Sandbury's mermaid said, gesturing to a carriage that looked like it was made of solid gold.

Beattie dived in, taking the spot at the very front.

'No,' Nolla said. 'We sit in the front. Meri, *you* sit with us. Everyone else in the back.'

'Why do you think they like Meri the best?' Beattie said sadly. 'Meri doesn't even act like she likes them very much.'

Zelda narrowed her eyes. 'I have my suspicions.'

They took off, sailing elegantly right up through the centre of the shop to a shell-encrusted ceiling.

'We're going to hit it!' Zelda cried.

'Stop worrying, Zelda,' Beattie said, though she said it without taking her eyes off the ceiling.

'I'm a miracle,' Steve whispered. Which is what he often said when he thought he was going to die, because he really wanted those to be his last words.

'We're not going to *die*,' Beattie said, as the dolphins screeched to a halt, their noses perfectly pressed against the ceiling.

Zelda tapped one of them, as if checking to see if

they were broken. 'Are they faulty? They've taken us to the ceiling.'

'They're telling me that this is the way to Figgy Bass's VIP section,' Mimi explained.

'Oooh,' Beattie said. 'I've never seen *anyone* go to Figgy Bass's studio – I had no idea it was hidden up here!'

The ceiling shells began to flash. Every mermaid in the store looked up.

'We're the reason it's flashing,' Nolla called down to them. 'Not,' she pointed at the others, '*these* mermaids. They are simply our GLAM squad.'

A huge shell on the ceiling flipped open and the dolphins sailed through, past racks of glittering clothes, before coming to a stop in front of Figgy Bass.

Beattie and the others had watched her many times on *Catwalk Prawn* – she was one of the judges and very difficult to please.

'Oh, you fabulous pair!' Figgy Bass oozed as they all got out of the sleigh. 'And you've brought some friends.'

'Not friends, more like servants,' Vetty said.

 73

'We're *assistants*,' Meri said, clearly trying to swallow her fury. '*ASSISTANTS*.'

'Well,' Figgy Bass said, plonking a pile of clothes on top of Meri. 'You can assist the Sushi Sisters in trying on outfits. That one on top is so unique it doesn't even look like an item of clothing.'

Zelda was handed an assortment of handbags because she was technically in charge of clothing and accessories.

'Don't drop *any of them*,' Figgy Bass said. 'I haven't glued all the embellishments on yet and a single grain of sand will *ruin* them.'

Beattie watched from across the room as Zelda wobbled from left to right.

And dropped one!

Beattie closed her eyes and swished her tail. She had promised not to do magic, but it was an emergency!

The bag leapt up and hooked itself on to Zelda's little finger.

When Beattie opened her eyes, the Sushi Sisters were looking at her.

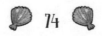

'Whoops, that was close!' Zelda said loudly, her tail shaking with a mix of fear and fury. Then she raced over to Beattie.

'You did magic! What did we say about using your magic?' she fretted. 'It's a secret, Beattie, you have to keep it under wraps.'

'Yes, you're very welcome that I saved you from getting into trouble with Figgy Bass,' Beattie said. 'No one saw me.'

'The Sushi Sisters were looking in your direction,' Zelda hissed.

'*No one saw me*,' Beattie said. 'You really need to stop worrying so much, Zelda.'

Zelda flicked her tail angrily and looked ready to burst, but something Nolla was saying distracted her.

'Yes, *leggings*.'

Zelda weaved closer. She could see Meri was eagerly listening too.

'You know, clothing with the bits for *legs*,' Nolla whispered.

Figgy Bass nodded. '*Well*,' she said, glancing around

to check no one was listening. (Zelda was the closest, but she pretended to inspect a hat.) 'When I was at Rupert Razorclam's School of Mermaid Fashion, we made human clothes for fun, so you have asked the right mermaid! When do you need them?'

'As soon as possible,' Vetty said. She handed Figgy Bass a scrap of seaweed with the design she was looking for drawn on it. 'Our plans have accelerated. Everything has slotted into place.'

Meri and Zelda exchanged worried glances.

'What's she saying?' Meri mouthed.

'Oh, I like the sushi print and tartan trim,' Figgy Bass said. 'I'll send them via Sandbury dolphin later this evening.'

'Perfect,' Vetty said with a smirk.

Zelda waited until they were back in the bustling main section of Sandbury's before speaking to Meri.

'Now they're buying human clothes? They definitely think they can get to land.'

'My thoughts exactly,' Meri said. 'There must be something we're missing. We need to get a better idea of their plan if we're going to stop them.'

'I know!' Zelda said. 'We should find out where human leggings with a sushi print and tartan trim are popular. They'll want to blend in. The leggings will help us narrow our search to a few key human areas.'

Meri smiled weakly and thought how useful the World Wardrobe class would have been for this situation.

'So …' Zelda said. 'Do the leggings provide any clues?'

12

Beattie Becomes a Sushi Sister

Back in the fishvan, all Meri and Zelda could think about was leggings.

'What's tartan?' Zelda whispered. 'I wonder if that's significant at all?'

'I'll see if there's any information about it on my clam compact,' Meri said, as she reached under her pillow to get it.

She felt around, expecting her fingers to hit on its hard shell. She dived another hand under, then her head.

'Everything all right, Meri?' Zelda asked as the mermaid disappeared under her pillow.

'No!' Meri cried, flipping her entire bunk upside down.

'WHAT ARE YOU DOING?' Beattie yelled.

'My clam compact,' Meri said urgently. 'You know,

the one with secret Fortress Bay things on it? It's gone! But it can't have, I just had it.'

'That's awful,' Mimi chirped from the corner.

They all looked over to see her covered in small tubes and shells.

'*Mimi*,' Zelda said. 'What are you *doing*?'

'Making a playground for the hamstars – I'm connecting lots of tubes for them to swim around in.'

'It was right here,' Meri said, as she turned the whole room upside down.

'You probably put it somewhere else,' Beattie said from her bunk, where she was lying flat out, arms behind her head, as if she were sunbathing on a lilo in Pinkly Lagoon.

'I bet the Sushi Sisters took it!' Zelda growled.

Beattie sat bolt upright. 'Zelda, what is your problem? Why would the Sushi Sisters do something like that? You're so mean to them.'

'What?' Zelda spluttered. 'You can't see what's right in front of you because you're blinded by all the fame and SUSHI.'

'Sushi comes from a human place called Japan,' Mimi chirped from the corner. 'It's my dream to go on holiday there one day. Apparently, it's even more beautiful than the mermaid kingdom of Mume.'

'That's nice, Mimi,' Zelda said through gritted teeth, as Mimi floated out of the door with an armful of tubes. 'But right now we're dealing with A VERY SERIOUS PROBLEM!'

'It's hardly serious,' Beattie laughed.

'Meri and I know things you don't,' Zelda said. 'Beattie, you have to trust me! The Sushi Sisters are *bad*. The crabagram is *true*.'

Beattie rolled her eyes. 'What makes you think that?'

'Well, shoes,' Zelda said. 'They have shoes.'

'Shoes?' Beattie said, faking concern. 'How *criminal*.'

'They're strange things to own if you're a mermaid,' Zelda protested.

'You own lots of human shoes!' Beattie cried.

'Yeah,' Zelda said. 'But they're odd shoes and old ones and I use them for shockey pucks. These shoes were brand new, and matching *pairs*.'

'They are also getting Figgy Bass to make them human clothes,' Meri said. 'Leggings, to be specific – which would require legs. We think they're going to get legs in order to fulfil their plan of destroying the humans.'

'Really?' Beattie said. 'That's all you've got? And how are they going to destroy the humans?'

Meri and Zelda looked at each other.

'A … destruction … machine?' Zelda mumbled.

'You don't have anything!' Beattie said. 'I thought you were Fortress Bay's best spy, Meri? And I thought you were better than this, Zelda. I think you're jealous because the Sushi Sisters are having fun and you're bored and sad because your shockey team didn't pick you for shockey camp.'

'*Beattie*,' Zelda said in disbelief. It wasn't like Beattie to tell secrets she had promised to keep.

'She didn't even get picked for the shockey team this season,' Beattie said to Meri. 'Rachel Rocker, her teammate and shockey best friend, said she wasn't good enough any more.'

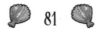

'Oh, Zelda,' Meri said, floating closer to her. 'I'm so sorry.'

Zelda tried to smile, but it was obvious she was hurt. 'It doesn't matter,' she said quietly. 'I missed some practice sessions because I was busy saving the world with all of you, but I couldn't tell her that! It's a secret. She said my shockey skills had slipped. She's not a bad friend, she was just doing the best for the team.'

'Zelda was furious,' Beattie added.

'ONLY INITIALLY!' Zelda protested. 'Now I see her point.'

'Zelda is jealous of the Sushi Sisters because they're doing exactly what they love!'

'That's a bit far-fetched,' Zelda scoffed.

'Not as far-fetched as the Sushi Sisters destroying all the humans,' Beattie said. She swam angrily to Meri's bunk.

'What are you doing?' Meri asked, just as Beattie yanked out something wedged down the side.

'*See*,' Beattie said, producing the clamshell compact. 'It was here all along.'

Just then the door to their bunk room was flung open. The Sushi Sisters floated in the hallway, hands on hips.

'We're inviting our favourite to a sleepover,' they said at once. 'SUSH!'

Zelda rolled her eyes.

'Oh that sounds like great fun,' Meri muttered.

'No, not you,' the Sushi Sisters said. 'Beattie.'

'But, I thought—' Meri began.

Beattie didn't hesitate. She gathered up her star hair clip, seaweed pillow and Steve's false teeth, which he had smuggled back into the fishvan.

'Not Steve,' the Sushi Sisters said.

Beattie placed the teeth back down on the bunk.

'Get rid of them,' Vetty said.

'But that's my *bedroom*,' Steve said.

'I think he just said sush,' Nolla said with a glint in her eye.

'I did NOT say sush!' Steve cried. 'Well, I said sush just then, oh and again now. Sush, Steve! I mean SHUSH. Oh …'

'You said the forbidden word, so I'm afraid you're banned from the fishvan,' Vetty said. 'Please leave and take the false teeth with you.'

'That's not fair!' Zelda cried. 'Poor Steve didn't say it until you did.'

'But that's the thing,' Nolla argued. 'We're allowed to say it and *he* isn't.'

'It's a nonsense rule,' Zelda huffed.

Beattie floated in silence as Steve stared up at her.

'Sorry, Steve,' she said. 'You broke the rules, so you'll have to go.'

They all watched as Steve floated sadly out of the door.

'One more thing, Beattie!' Vetty said. 'We've decided that *you* are going to *be* a Sushi Sister. You'll be on the show for our final two pranks!'

'WHAT?' Beattie said breathlessly. '*Me?* A *Sushi Sister?*'

'You'll be famous, just like us. And the last prank will show that you truly *are* a Sushi Sister,' Vetty said, making Nolla giggle.

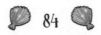

'What does that mean?' Zelda asked.

The Sushi Sisters each put an arm around Beattie.

'Come on, Beattie. You're *our* friend now.'

The door closed with a loud bang.

'You don't think they're going to get Beattie involved in their terrible plan, do you?' Zelda said. 'Beattie is very determined not to be herself – would new Beattie destroy all the humans?'

 85

'I was thinking the same thing,' Meri said gravely. 'And for what it's worth, Zelda, I know this has nothing to do with the fact you weren't picked for the shockey team or because you didn't get to go to shockey camp. The Sushi Sisters are fishy, without a doubt. But one thing Beattie said is true – I am supposed to be the best spy mermaid in Fortress Bay. It's time to start acting like it.'

'Yeah!' Zelda said, punching the air. 'What are you going to do first?'

Meri flipped open the clam compact. 'I'm going to call Sabrina and ask if she knows what tartan is.'

13

Sabrina Is on Holiday

Sabrina was on holiday and so Meri's call was diverted to the Teenies, Meri's triplet bunkmates back at spy school.

'A holiday is something to do with inflatable things floating on water, if we remember that class we took on How to Be Less Fortress Bay and More Normal,' the Teenies said airily, and in unison. They always said the same thing at the same time.

'I know what a holiday is!' Meri said. 'I just can't believe Sabrina would take one.'

'Oh, has she taken it from someone? Are holidays something you steal?' the Teenies asked, still clearly unsure of what a holiday was. They never listened in lessons and often copied Meri's homework.

Meri slapped her hand to her head. 'NEVER MIND!'

'Anything else?' the Teenies asked.

'Do you know what tartan is?' Meri asked flatly, feeling almost certain they wouldn't.

'It's a fabric with a criss-cross pattern that is most commonly associated with Scotland.'

Meri's mouth fell open.

'Is that everything?' they asked.

'You're sure?' Meri said excitedly. 'You're sure it's to do with Scotland?'

'Yes,' the Teenies said with an impatient sigh. 'We covered it in World Wardrobe class.'

Meri snapped the clamshell compact closed. 'Another piece of the puzzle. The Sushi Sisters' evil plan will take place in Scotland.'

'Paris,' Zelda said, her eyes growing wide. 'She's in Scotland!'

Mimi drifted into the room with the hamstars in her hair and a tube with eyes floating at her side.

'What,' Zelda said, 'is *that*?'

'It's Steve,' Mimi whispered. 'In a hamstar tube. I felt sorry for him, so I found a way to sneak him

back into the fishvan.'

'Hello, it's me,' Steve whispered.

'Yes, I can quite clearly see your eyes,' Zelda said.

'It's the perfect disguise!' Mimi cheered. 'A talking tube with eyes! The Sushi Sisters won't be suspicious at all.'

14

Coral

Back on land, Paris plopped her legs into the loch and gripped the crystal charm on her necklace, readying herself to investigate this strange ghost.

The little sea creatures inside her necklace looked up at her expectantly, wondering which of them she'd pick. Would it be the shark? The crocodile? The dolphin? The jellyfish? The mermaid? The number of shakes determined which creature she would become.

She looked around, to check no one was watching, then shook the necklace. With a swift *ffflllissp*, her long legs clad in her trademark knee-high socks morphed into a shimmering white tail.

Paris slipped into the cold, still water.

She swam down, deeper and deeper, pushing through reams of seaweed and nodding at eels as she went.

It wasn't long before she spotted something strange –
the clump of coral that she had seen the ghostly boy
wearing was floating on the spot. She tried to move it,
but it wouldn't budge.

'But that's impossible,' she said to no one. 'How can
something float in water and be unmovable?'

She swam around it, tapping her chin in thought.

'Fine!' Paris said. 'If there's no one here, I'm going
home.'

She turned, pretending to leave.

'No, wait!' came a voice and, as if by magic, a ghostly-
looking boy appeared, the coral perfectly crowning his
head.

'AAAAAAAARGHHHH!' Paris cried, racing over to
an eel cave and trying to hide inside.

The boy was growing clearer and moving closer.

'Don't be afraid,' he whispered.

'DON'T BE AFRAID?!' Paris roared, as all around
her amazing creatures began to appear.

She spun in frantic circles as mercats and weird
hamster-starfish hybrids danced around her.

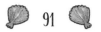

'THIS CAN'T BE REAL!' she cried.

The mermaid boy with his seal tail and coral crown floated quietly in front of her.

Windows began to appear in the rocks and cave houses, shops and clam cars materialised out of nowhere, as if she'd just woken up an ancient, sleeping city.

'I was hoping you'd find us,' he said. 'I'm sorry if my giggling scared you. I was laughing at the Flubiére fish.'

'You're a ghost!' Paris said, looking around her in amazement.

'I am not,' the boy said, sounding more than a little offended. 'I'm just pale.'

'I'm Paris,' Paris said nervously. 'I'm sorry I thought you were a ghost.'

'That's no problem at all,' the boy said. 'Welcome to Corloch, an ancient, forgotten mermaid city. I am Coral Skye, the only mermaid who swims here now.'

'Coral?' Paris said.

'It's Mermaid for Carl. You're not a real mermaid, are you?' he said, his eyes shifting to Paris's necklace. 'You're a human with a magic necklace.'

Paris nodded. 'I sometimes morph into a mermaid. The necklace was given to me by a mermaid queen, I promise I didn't steal it. I have mermaid friends – real ones. Real mermaids, I mean. And they're real friends too. But they live far away now, and I don't think I'm going to see much of them any more.'

A mercat floated past and settled itself on Coral's shoulder.

'Why are there so many of these weird half-and-half creatures here?' Paris asked, as a crabbit hopped past.

'I created them!' Coral said. 'I invented them all. If you see one anywhere in the world, it was created right here. I'm an inventor! They pop back to the loch every now and then to visit me – when they're on land they morph into normal creatures, like cats with legs.'

'That's so cool! I'm an inventor too!' Paris said. 'I call myself the Gadget Queen. But I don't really invent any more, not since I got this magic necklace – it's the greatest invention of all time! It doesn't feel like there's any point in inventing anything else.'

'It's only the greatest because you haven't invented anything better yet. Don't stop! Especially if you find it fun! Sometimes I think I've created the greatest creature in the world – I definitely thought that when I invented merkittens – but then I invented hamstars, and they're EVEN BETTER.'

Paris smiled. She liked Coral a lot.

 94

'Then perhaps you could help me.' She handed Coral the clamshell compact. 'Two inventors have to be better than one – I need to fix this clam compact so I can speak to my mermaid friends.'

'Of course!' Coral said kindly. 'Leave it with me. Oh, and can I ask your opinion on a new creature idea?'

'Yes, of course,' Paris replied.

'What do you think of a CHARK?'

Paris paused for a moment. 'Is it half chicken, half shark?'

'It is!' Coral replied.

'I don't think the world needs that, Coral.'

The Tartan Times

Today, while on a birthday fishing trip, Callum McBroth caught a very strange fish indeed.

REPORTER: Callum, what happened?

CALLUM McBROTH: I caught the wee fish, and then it started putting lipstick on me.

REPORTER: Did the fish have a name?

CALLUM McBROTH: It wasn't a talking fish! Or if it was, it was very quiet.

REPORTER: I understand you purchased the lipstick. Did the fish sell it to you?

CALLUM McBROTH: No, it just put it on for me. A woman called Susan Silkensocks appeared in front of us and said it was mermaid make-up and she was the only human in the world allowed to sell it.

REPORTER: Sorry, did you just say mermaid make-up? Surely you don't believe that?!

CALLUM McBROTH: I've just had a pufferfish put lipstick on me, I'm starting to believe everything.

REPORTER: Thank you, Callum McBroth!

Yesterday, this sleepy town had only a ghost mermaid to boast about, but today it looks like we've got pufferfish selling mermaid make-up too! And everyone thought the Loch Ness Monster was weird …

15

Zelda Leaves the Fishvan

It was time to leave the Hidden Lagoon and set off for the location of the next prank. Mermaids all the way from Anchor Rock to Oysterdale couldn't wait to find out where the Sushi Sisters would pop up next. But inside the fishvan, the news was already out.

'We're going to Salmon City?' Zelda choked. 'But that's near *Scotland.*'

'Is it?' Nolla said, trying not to smile.

Meri and Zelda looked at each other knowingly.

'Why are you looking at each other like that?' Beattie asked. She knew Zelda well enough to know it was suspicious.

The Sushi Sisters had given her a makeover, so she had bright orange nail polish and a cap covered in hamstar stickers.

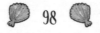

'Nice hat,' Zelda said, to distract her. 'Did you make that at your sleepover?' 'I did actually,' Beattie said. 'Are you jealous?'

'Not of the hat,' Zelda muttered under her breath.

'I don't like this,' Mimi said, throwing her Sandcrackle cereal at the wall. Everyone floated in shocked silence. Mimi had never been angry before, and she'd *never* wasted Sandcrackle cereal.

'Are you feeling all right, Mi—' Zelda began, but her twin cut her off.

'I'M NOT FINISHED!' she cried. 'We have always got along – it's always been the three of us, Beattie, Mimi and Zelda, and we pick up friends along the way because we're great. I don't know why you're fighting and I'm sick of it. It's making me sad.'

Zelda put a comforting hand on her sister's shoulder. 'The reason we're fighting,' she whispered, 'is because Beattie is being HORRIBLE.'

Beattie rolled her eyes.

'Beattie is a Sushi Sister now,' Nolla said with a wry smile.

'And so you're fired,' Vetty said, flicking her tail in Zelda's face. 'You're not coming to Salmon City with us.'

'Where should we drop you off?' Nolla asked. 'The shockey stadium? Oh, no, wait – you're not playing any more, are you?'

Zelda stared at Beattie in disbelief. 'You told *them* my shockey secret too? You're meant to be my friend, but because you'd rather be cool like the Sushi Sisters, you're being mean to everyone else. I don't want to be friends with someone like that.'

Beattie didn't know what to say. She and Zelda often bickered, but this felt serious.

Zelda grabbed her bags and swam angrily to the

door. 'Good luck, Meri Pebble,' she said. 'You're going to need it.'

She slammed the door shut, but not before giving Meri a little wink.

'What did the wink mean?' Meri whispered urgently to Mimi, but Mimi wasn't listening. She handed the Sushi Sisters their hamstars.

'Zelda is my sister,' Mimi said. 'So …'

And with that she quietly left too.

'Ugh, this is a problem,' the Sushi Sisters said. 'Now there's no one to look after the hamstars. Where's that annoying seahorse when you need him?'

A little tube floated out of the Sandcrackle cereal box.

'I will *happily* look after your hamstars,' Steve said quickly, not wanting to leave Beattie at the mercy of the Sushi Sisters.

'I can't believe they left,' Beattie said. 'Maybe we can get them to come back?'

'You don't need them, silly!' Nolla said. 'You have us now.'

Meri began gathering up the bowls from breakfast, muttering furiously under her breath. Her heart was beating in her mouth. Zelda and Mimi were gone and she was alone to finish the mission. The Sushi Sisters were headed towards Scotland and she still had to figure out the details of their evil plan. The fate of every human rested *IN HER HANDS*!

A fish pushed past, knocking the breakfast bowls from her grasp.

'BUT MY HANDS CAN'T EVEN HOLD BOWLS!' she wailed.

16

Charks, Again

The next morning, once her mother had set off to buy party supplies, Paris ran to the loch and dived in.

This time Coral was waiting for her.

They swam around the deserted city, ducking in and out of ancient houses, followed by a trail of mercats and crabbits.

'Do you ever get lonely here?' Paris asked.

'Sometimes,' he said with a hint of sadness in his voice. 'The other mermaids moved to Salmon City a long time ago. My grandmother told me about this place, she said it would be the perfect spot for inventing weird and wonderful creatures. She used to invent them too. In fact, one of her greatest creations is still hiding in a loch nearby.'

'What kind of creature is it?' Paris asked excitedly.

'It's a dragon-and-eel combination,' Coral said. 'The humans call him Nessie. He's actually quite famous now. Oh, I have something you might like to try!'

He rushed off and returned with two battered old tin mugs filled with juice. 'Seaweed Slimer?' he asked. 'Mixed it myself.'

'Thank you,' Paris said, politely taking the mug, though she wasn't convinced she wanted to drink it. 'Coral, I have a question.'

'Is it about CHARKS?' Coral asked hopefully.

'No,' Paris said. 'How do you make yourself invisible? Yesterday, when we met, the whole city was invisible at first, and all the creatures in it, including you. How did you do that?'

'Do you know what cephalopods are? It's a tricky word if you don't speak Mermaid.'

'Seflapod?' Paris said, saying it how it sounded.

'It's a group of sea creatures, including the octopus and the squid,' Coral said, gulping down his Seaweed Slimer. 'And one of the things cephalopods can do is change the colour of their bodies so they are completely camouflaged. This whole area, every loch and patch of seawater north of Salmon City, behaves like an octopus or a squid – anything in this water right here can become camouflaged.'

Paris was impressed. She took a sip of her Seaweed Slimer and spat it straight out.

'What about mermaids with octopus tails?' she asked, hoping Coral wouldn't fill up her mug. 'Do they have special camouflage powers?'

'Unfortunately, no,' Coral said. 'Mermaids with octopus tails can't camouflage themselves. You have to be pure cephalopod or live in these waters to do it.'

'Can I do it?' Paris asked excitedly.

'Of course,' Coral said. 'Just wish you were invisible.'

Paris lay back on the rock and wished and wished. Within seconds she disappeared.

'Bravo!' Coral said, clapping.

Paris wished to be seen again, and all of a sudden she was visible.

'What other things can an octopus do?' she asked, keen to try more tricks.

'They can squeeze through small spaces the size of their eye!'

'That doesn't sound as fun,' Paris said.

'They can also read minds!' Coral went on. 'That's why so many mermaids have octopus assistants – they know what you want before you ask for it!'

'But I can't read your mind,' Paris said.

'Yes you can!' Coral said with a smile. 'Haven't you noticed we've been having this whole conversation in our heads?'

Paris tumbled backwards. He was right, their mouths hadn't moved at all.

'Now,' Coral said, picking up her clam compact. 'Why don't we have a go at fixing this so you can reach your friends.'

Paris grinned.

Little did she know, her friends were on their way.

17

Mermaids on a Plane

Back in Mimi and Zelda's bedroom in Periwinkle Palace, the twins were making a plan.

'We've got to go to Scotland and warn Paris she's in danger,' Zelda said, swimming in nervous circles.

'We should head for Salmon City then,' Mimi said. 'That's the closest we can get to Paris's new castle.'

Zelda shook her head and bit at her nails. 'No, the Sushi Sisters are already on their way there. We need to beat them to it.'

'But how do we get to Scotland before them?' Mimi asked, her eyes fixed on the latest episode of *Clippee*.

'We need legs,' Zelda said. 'We'll get to the closest bit of land, which is California, and then we'll take human transport to Scotland. Then we'll be ready and waiting to stop them by the time they arrive.'

'Arabella Cod is not going to give us legs,' Mimi said. 'We've done our summer on land. And I don't think she'll believe the story about the Sushi Sisters.'

Zelda grinned. 'Look around, Mimi. We *live* in Periwinkle Palace, who else lives here?'

'Our parents and all the other mermaids who work for Arabella Cod. And Arabella Cod herself.'

'Exactly. I'll just forge a legs permission slip,' Zelda said with a shrug. 'They're in Arabella Cod's throne room. It'll take me five minutes.'

'You can't forge a permission slip!' Mimi said. 'Well, you can, but you *shouldn't*. It would be *bad*.'

Zelda hovered above the TV for a moment to consider it. 'I think the worst thing would be to sit here watching *Clippee* cartoons while the Sushi Sisters destroy all the humans.'

'You're right,' Mimi said.

Zelda sighed. 'I always am.'

Forging the permission slip was easy. And so was getting to land. The difficult part came when they reached the airport.

'We need to get to Paris,' Zelda said, slamming some human money down on the desk.

'Where did you get that?' Mimi whispered.

'The permission slip had a section asking how much money was required. I guessed. I could only remember that *billion* is an amount.'

The desk attendant looked down her nose at them. 'Two tickets to Paris … yes, I can arrange that.'

Zelda jumped up and down. 'It's lucky she knows where Paris is.'

'France,' the desk attendant said.

'Pardon?' Zelda replied.

'Paris is in France.'

'No,' Zelda said slowly. 'Paris is in Scotland.'

The desk attendant looked confused. 'I'm afraid Paris is definitely in France.'

'You don't need to be afraid, because Paris is definitely in Scotland,' Mimi joined in.

'Paris is in *France*,' the desk attendant said, sounding a little impatient.

'Scotland.'

'France.'

'Scotland.'

'FRANCE.'

'SCOTLAND.'

'DO YOU JUST WANT TWO TICKETS TO SCOTLAND THEN?' the desk assistant roared, making everyone and everything screech to a halt.

'Yes please,' Zelda said sweetly.

Five minutes later ...

'Which way to the tin whales?' Mimi shouted into the crowds. 'Anyone know where we find our tin whale?'

An elderly gentleman stopped beside her with an amused look on his face.

'I think you mean aeroplane,' he said.

'Oh!' Mimi said, patting the man on the shoulder. 'Is that what he's called?'

'Who?' the man asked.

'Our tin whale! Thank you for letting me know he's called Aeroplane,' she said with a bow before skipping off to find her twin.

Sometime after that …

On board the plane, Zelda was feeling worried again.

'Just wanted to check,' she whispered to the flight attendant. 'Is this one called Aeroplane?'

The flight attendant stared blankly at her. 'Yes.'

'Oh good!' Zelda said with a sigh of relief. 'There were so many tin whales I really wanted to make sure we got the right one!'

18

Meanwhile, in the Mermaid World…

'The FISHHAM BIT ME, BEATTIE! THE FISHHAM!'

'Steve, I think you mean *hamstar*.'

'I don't think I do, but fine – THE FISHHAM HAMSTARRED ME!'

19

The Salmon-Pink Shipwreck

Meri peered out of the window. They had left the safety of the Hidden Lagoon and were in the Upper Realms. She flipped open her clamshell compact to check for human divers and boats.

'We're safe for now,' she said. 'It won't be long until we get to Salmon City.'

Steve – still stuck in his tube – floated next to her in silence.

'It's lonely without them,' Meri said. 'I bet they're back at Periwinkle Palace, watching *Clippee* cartoons and drinking foam shakes and having a lovely time. And I'm here, saving the humans.'

The fishvan began to slow and crowds of salmon gathered outside it.

The way into Salmon City was as secret and secure as

any other mermaid kingdom in the world. All you had to do was find the salmon-pink sunken ship.

Up at the front of the fishvan, Beattie leaned closer to the window to get a better look.

Salmon crowded the old, rusted ship's bow, but behind it there was nothing for miles. She couldn't understand where the city could be.

'Someone needs to board the ship and turn the wheel,' Nolla said, shoving Beattie towards the door.

Outside, the water was icy-cold and the sunken ship groaned. Beattie glided down through the captain's window to the wheel.

Normally, Beattie would have hesitated, worried about what might happen when she turned it, but she pushed the thought aside and got to work.

With every turn of the wheel, the ship floated higher and higher until she was level with the fishvan. She looked across to see the Sushi Sisters clapping excitedly as everything began to tremble.

'WHAT'S HAPPENING?!' Beattie shouted, as the groaning ship suddenly tipped forward and nosedived, disappearing into the seabed in a puff of sand.

All that remained was a gaping hole.

'Now for the best bit!' Vetty squealed.

A bubble floated up from the hole. Inside it, on pink seaweed ribbons, was the city's famous message:

WELCOME TO SALMON CITY! THE GLITZIEST, FISHIEST CITY IN THIS BIT OF SEA!

Then came Beattie. She clawed her way out of the hole and spat sand out of her mouth.

'Oh thank cods!' Steve cried. 'She's lost that awful hat.'

'Well done, Beattie,' Vetty said, patting her on the back. 'Everyone knows opening the gate to Salmon City is horrible. You were so good to volunteer.'

'I didn't,' Beattie said, still spitting sand. 'And I wouldn't have done it if I'd known there was quite so much sand.' She coughed and a baby salmon fell out of her mouth. 'And fish.'

'It's Salmon City,' Nolla said. 'Of course there's fish!'

They all stared into the hole at the bustling city deep beneath them.

'Come on,' Vetty said. 'The hole will close up soon. Everyone in the fishvan, I'll steer us down.'

 117

Hidden deep under a sandy seabed, Salmon City was mostly made up of clumps of pebbly mermaid houses. Fish and mismatched clam cars zoomed past and bright lights from apartments illuminated the rocky avenues.

'Where are you doing your prank?' Beattie asked, as Meri gathered the filming equipment from the fishvan.

An elderly mermaid inched past. She was so old she was barely able to swim. The Sushi Sisters watched her like a shark watches its next meal.

It didn't take a spy to figure out what they were thinking.

'You can't play a prank on that old mermaid,' Meri said in disbelief. 'That's just mean.'

The Sushi Sisters giggled.

'It's Wendy Krill,' Nolla said.

'Krill?' Beattie said. The name sounded familiar to her.

Meri's eyes narrowed. 'It's Wigbert Krill's mother, isn't it?'

The Sushi Sisters nodded excitedly.

 119

'But she doesn't have a moustache to shave off,' Steve pointed out.

'What have you got against Wigbert Krill and his family?' Meri demanded.

'Nothing,' the Sushi Sisters said together. 'SUSH!'

'We thought it would be poetic,' Vetty said. 'First we prank Wigbert Krill and it makes us famous, and then for our penultimate prank of the series we PRANK HIS MOTHER!'

'We love a theme,' Nolla said, fiddling with her sushi earrings. 'It's important to have a theme sometimes. Have you ever been to a birthday party without a theme? It's HORRENDOUS.'

'Isn't the theme of a birthday party THAT IT'S SOMEONE'S BIRTHDAY?' Meri said, trying to remain composed but failing.

'No, it needs to be something like SPARKLE or MERPETS to be a theme,' Vetty said. 'Birthday is not a theme.'

Beattie was glad Zelda wasn't around to hear the conversation, because she hated nothing more than a

themed birthday party. She and Mimi argued about it every year. Mimi always wanted a *Clippee*-themed birthday party. Zelda always wanted a birthday-themed birthday party.

'I think birthday is a theme,' Beattie said.

'WILL EVERYONE STOP TALKING ABOUT THEMES?!' Meri roared. She coughed and regained her composure. 'What prank have you got planned for Wendy Krill?'

'Oh, it's so funny,' Vetty said. 'And Meri, we'll need your help for this one.'

20

The Fish-Slap Shower

Anyone who has ever been to one of the many hidden mermaid cities around the world will know that a fish-slap shower is a common feature in underwater bathrooms.

'We're going to slime her,' Vetty explained, as she handed Meri a shell full of green goo.

'And you're going to be the one to do it,' Nolla said.

Outside the fishvan, Salmon City mermaids were gathering in great clumps, excitedly awaiting the start of the show.

Meri looked at the growing audience outside. 'Oh no, I think one of you two should,' she said, trying to hand the slime back.

'No,' Vetty said sternly. 'It has to be you. We'll be outside the fishvan with Beattie, distracting Wendy

Krill, and then you will leap out and slime her when you hear the magic word.'

'Where will I leap out from?' Meri asked.

Nolla pointed to the bathroom. 'You'll hide in the fish-slap shower, then burst out of the top.'

Meri floated inside. It was cramped and smelled of 'SUSH – the Sushi Sisters' limited-edition perfume. Above her she could see the hole where the fish filed in to slap any stray seaweed or sand off a mermaid's tail.

'Will I fit through here?' Meri asked, squeezing her head past the hole.

'Of course!' Nolla called up. 'Plenty of room!'

'So you'll wait in there until you hear us say the magic word, then squeeze out as quickly as possible, and slime Wendy Krill,' Vetty explained.

'She doesn't look like she wants to,' Nolla said.

'I do!' Meri said quickly, even though she didn't. There was no other option but to play along. 'What's the magic word?'

'Sush!' the Sushi Sisters and Beattie said together.

'Of course,' Meri groaned.

Meri heard the commotion outside – the sound of the Sushi Sisters shouting 'GLOWFISH! SHELL CAMERA! ACTION!' and the screams from the crowd as they introduced Beattie as the third Sushi Sister.

But then everything went very quiet.

'They're probably waiting for Wendy Krill,' Meri whispered to Steve, who was floating in his tube next to her.

A clam car fired up outside, making a loud *put-putting* noise.

'Who do you suppose that is?' Meri murmured. 'Maybe it's Wendy Krill. I'm sure I can hear the occasional whisper. How long have we been in here?'

'Over an hour,' Steve said.

'You don't think it's a trick, do you?' Meri asked. Her spy senses were tingling with the possibility. 'What if they locked me in here so they could get my clam compact, pretend to be me and request legs—'

'Your clam compact is floating right there,' Steve said, knocking it up to her face.

'Oh,' Meri said sheepishly.

She flipped it open.

'I keep checking to see if any permission slips for legs have gone through, but they haven't. If they had, it would be noted right here and—'

She gasped.

'DID THEY GET LEGS?' Steve cried, as he watched the colour drain from Meri's face.

'No, they didn't,' Meri said, sounding confused. 'But Zelda and Mimi did.'

'I bet they went to warn Paris. She's in Scotland, after all. They're still helping you!' Steve cheered. 'My mermaids never let anyone down.'

Meri smiled. 'That's why Zelda winked when she left the fishvan!'

'So if you've got a firm grip on your clam compact and that's the only way to get permission for legs,' Steve mused, 'and we're here in Salmon City, far from Arabella Cod, the only other mermaid who can grant permission for legs, then how are the Sushi Sisters going to get them?'

Meri's clamshell compact jiggled.

 125

'Hello?' she whispered.

'Ah, Meri!' came a cheery voice. 'It's been a while.'

'It's not the best time, Gronnyupple,' Meri said, grabbing hold of the shell of slime. 'I'm waiting for my cue to burst on to the Sushi Sisters' show. It's for a dangerous mission – involves legs and stuff. It's a long story, I'll tell you about it another time.'

'Oh, it sounds great fun!' Gronnyupple said. 'Just a quickie, I'm looking for Beattie, she was meant to send the latest magic for *Maritza Mist's Water Witch Catalogue*. I would make it myself, but she's the only water witch with the power to *make* magic, not just use it. I need her!'

Meri dropped the clamshell compact.

'Meri,' Steve said slowly. 'What's wrong?'

'Hello?' came Gronnyupple's voice. 'Beattie made an excellent new potion called Sweet Factory – all you do is sprinkle it on a sweet and it means every time you eat the sweet a new one appears! It lasts for days too. Hello … Meri?'

Meri shot up out of the shower, but got her tail

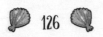

caught and she landed head first in the shell of slime.

To her surprise, a huge crowd erupted into laughter.

'That was their best prank yet!' a mermaid roared.

'I think Shower Mermaid is my favourite prank of all time!' another cried.

Meri wiped the slime from her eyes and looked at the crowd. They were all wearing Sushi Sisters T-shirts and jewellery and caps.

But the Sushi Sisters were nowhere to be seen.

'*What* did you do that for?' Steve asked, as the crowd swam off and the octopuses put away the cameras. 'Did we ruin the prank?'

'No,' Meri said. 'It went *exactly* how they wanted it to go. I see everything clearly now.'

'What did Gronnyupple say that made you freak out?' Steve asked.

'Beattie,' Meri said. 'She's magic.'

'In so many ways!' Steve said. 'But you already knew she was magic.'

'But it didn't cross my mind that she could use magic to give them legs!' Meri said, as all the pieces of the

 127

puzzle finally slotted into place. 'Oh it all makes sense! The Sushi Sisters sent the crabagram! They insisted that writing "THE SUSHI SISTERS ARE GOING TO DESTROY ALL THE HUMANS" would get picked up by spies.'

'But spies are a secret,' Steve said.

'Yes, but everyone imagines we exist somewhere,' Meri said. 'They just had to do a little fishing – put the message out there and see if we took the bait.'

'But,' Steve said, 'why would they want the message to get picked up by spies?'

'Because then a spy would be on to them. They fired their assistant knowing it would be perfect bait for a spy – the perfect cover to get close to them. And they were right – Sabrina sent me straight away. Their plan must have been to befriend me and convince me to get them legs, or steal my clam compact. But then I brought Beattie, and then she did magic at Sandbury's!'

'And Zelda *knew* the Sushi Sisters had seen her!' Steve cried.

'They must've,' Meri said. 'After Sandbury's, they

started calling Beattie their favourite. When they saw she was a water witch, they knew she was their best chance of getting legs – she's a Sushi Sister superfan who would do anything for them!'

'So you arrived to stop them and accidentally gave them everything they needed?' Steve said.

'Yes, thank you, Steve,' Meri said.

'So what are they going to do now?'

'Well, this was obviously a ploy to get me out of the way. They knew I was a spy all along,' Meri said. 'I'm glad Gronnyupple called or I would've been in that shower for days.'

'YOU'RE WELCOME!' came a voice from the clamshell compact. 'HAPPY TO HELP!'

'I think that clam car we heard was them speeding off to land,' Meri said. 'They're way ahead of us now.'

'What will they do when they get there?' Steve asked.

Meri stared off into the distance. 'Destroy all the humans. And they're starting in Scotland, where Paris is.'

Steve gasped. 'And where Zelda and Mimi are

currently pretending to be humans! What if Zelda and Mimi and Paris don't see them coming?'

'We need to get to land before the Sushi Sisters do,' Meri said.

'But it's impossible – we can't get there before them,' Steve said, as he started to hyperventilate with panic.

Meri winked. 'Don't worry, Steve, it's time I got some serious spy backup.' She pointed towards the Salmon City cinema.

'I'm not sure a trip to the cinema is going to help. Even if they are showing the film adaptation of *The Five Flops of Wanda Wetly*,' Steve said.

'It's the oldest mermaid cinema in the world,' Meri said. 'But it's never *just* been a cinema …'

The Tartan Times

Today we interviewed Susan Silkensocks, new castle owner and the woman behind the Flubiére make-up brand. Tonight she is hosting a party at her home to meet the locals, and we can't wait!

REPORTER: Susan Silkensocks, please can you explain why the Flubiére make-up brand is promoted using pufferfish?

SUSAN SILKENSOCKS: The mermaids are responsible for all that stuff. I just sell it.

REPORTER: Not real mermaids though?

SUSAN SILKENSOCKS: Yes, real ones. The pufferfish are trained by them to apply the make-up. It's all very professional.

REPORTER: And you get the pufferfish and the make-up from … ?

SUSAN SILKENSOCKS: *MERMAIDS!*

REPORTER: But not real mermaids?

SUSAN SILKENSOCKS: Of course they're real. There's no such thing as a FAKE mermaid.

REPORTER: What about a human who dresses up as a mermaid?

SUSAN SILKENSOCKS: That's a human dressed up as a mermaid, not a fake mermaid.

REPORTER: What about a statue of a mermaid?

SUSAN SILKENSOCKS: That's a statue.

REPORTER: A chocolate shaped like a mermaid?

SUSAN SILKENSOCKS: That's a bit of chocolate, not a fake mermaid! No one has ever eaten a bit of chocolate shaped like a mermaid and said, 'Mmm, fake mermaid.'

REPORTER: So you genuinely think mermaids are real? What about the ghost mermaid who lives in your loch?

133

SUSAN SILKENSOCKS: Oh, that one is made up. Ghosts aren't real.

REPORTER: Everyone in this town believes in the ghost mermaid.

SUSAN SILKENSOCKS: Well, everyone here is SILLY. Come to my party!

21

Flubiérarty

Paris and Coral had no luck fixing the clamshell compact, but he had promised to keep trying.

Sure enough, when Paris went to her room later that evening to get changed for the party, there was a parcel waiting on her bed. A soggy one, wrapped in seaweed.

She leaned out of her open window and saw Coral in the loch below.

'How did you get this up here?' Paris cried.

'THREW IT!' he shouted back.

Paris was just marvelling at his ability to throw the parcel through a small open window, when she spotted the glass all over the floor and the huge hole in the other window.

'SORRY ABOUT THE WINDOW!' came Coral's voice from below.

 135

Paris ripped the parcel open. Her clam compact wasn't just fixed, it had been given a brand-new mercat-themed case. It looked better than ever.

She flipped it open and waited to see if it would connect to her mermaid friends.

There was a crackle, and a flash of tail on the screen. 'HELLO?' she shouted. 'HELLO?'

The picture grew clearer – it was the twins' bedroom in Periwinkle Palace! Only it seemed like no one was in. Shockey gear floated around the room, along with *Clamzine* magazines and a shell TV set playing *Clippee* cartoons.

'Mimi? Zelda? Beattie?' Paris said hopefully. 'Are you there?'

She waited a moment and then shoved the clam compact under her pillow.

'ANY LUCK?' came a cry from Coral.

'WHO. IS. SHOUTING. OUTSIDE. MY. HOOOOOOUSE?' roared Susan Silkensocks, throwing the door open just as Coral ducked under the water.

She looked up and saw Paris at the window. 'PARIS!

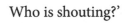

Who is shouting?'

'I think it's you,' Paris said, trying not to laugh.

'VERY FUNNY,' her mother snapped. 'Get ready. I need you downstairs to serve canapés. They are carrots shaped to look like mermaid tails and they were VERY EXPENSIVE.'

'Yes, yes,' Paris said, pulling on her party dress, but keeping her trademark knee-high socks on under it.

Downstairs, guests were starting to arrive – mostly fishermen in brightly coloured Flubiére make-up who seemed disturbed by the canapés.

'Each individual scale on the carrot was expertly carved,' Paris heard her mother saying. Paris quickly picked up a tray and began walking around the edge of the room.

'There will be a promotional pufferfish display in the loch a little later,' Paris could hear her mother

telling some guests. 'Like a firework display, but with fish wearing make-up.'

Paris took a break and shoved four of the carrot canapés in her mouth. She was just about to pick up the tray again when she spotted something outside the window. Something in the bushes that looked familiar. Something that looked a lot like –

Paris choked.

'I KNOW FIRST AID!' a fisherman bellowed, diving across the room and whacking Paris's back. The carrot

went flying across the room and hit Susan Silkensocks in the eye.

'MY FLUBIÉRE LASHES!' Susan Silkensocks howled, as they fell to the floor.

Paris raced out of the door and made a beeline for the bushes.

'Zelda! Mimi!' Paris cried, throwing herself at her mermaid friends and hugging them tightly. 'You're here! And you have *legs*.'

22

Carrots Shaped Like Mermaids

Luckily the castle was big enough to hide a couple of mermaids with legs, and the party was so busy no one noticed them sneaking in.

Paris brought them a tray of canapés and a glass of lemonade each.

'I saw all the people downstairs,' Zelda said, shoving carrots in her mouth. 'They look like they escaped from a Flubiére catalogue.'

'That's because Mother's been selling Flubiére to humans,' Paris said. 'I was sure she wouldn't sell a single lipstick. But tell me, how did you get here?'

'Tin whale!' Mimi cheered.

Paris looked surprised. 'You mean aeroplane?'

'Yes,' Zelda said. 'That *was* his name!'

'How did you buy tickets?' Paris said, biting

into a carrot.

'Forged a permission slip,' Zelda mumbled. 'Requested legs and money. Perhaps misjudged how much it would cost. I got us first-class plane tickets and I still have millions of pounds left over.'

Mimi flopped back on to the old sofa and a cloud of dust erupted around her. She began coughing madly.

'Other mermaids always say the worst thing about being a human is toes,' Zelda said. 'But I say it's this weird stuff.'

'Dust,' Paris said.

Zelda gagged. 'And I'd forgotten it smells so weird on land.'

'There's nothing nicer than the smell of seaweed and hundreds of fish!' Mimi chirped.

'That, my friends, is where we disagree,' Paris said, making them all laugh.

When Paris stopped laughing, she looked Zelda dead in the eye. 'Seriously, though – why are you here?'

'We're here because of the Sushi Sisters,' Zelda said. 'And trust me, they aren't as fun as they sound ...'

23

The Secret in the Salmon City Cinema

The Salmon City cinema was the oldest mermaid cinema in the world. It had shell seats and a big seaweed curtain in front of the screen, and it served sandbites on the backs of jellyfish. But there was one feature that made it unique: Coho, the cinema mascot.

Coho was really a mermaid called Trevor Trout dressed in a salmon costume. It was his job to greet every mermaid as they passed through the doors, help elderly mermaids swim to their seats, and clean up the sandbites people had spilled on the floor.

'See that mermaid dressed as a salmon?' Meri said, pointing Steve's tube in the direction of Coho. 'He's a Fortress Bay spy. He failed all his SPLATS – that's Spy Lessons and Tests – so they put him on

Salmon City cinema duty.'

'Well, he's doing a very good job because I had no idea he was a spy, I thought he was just a grumpy young mermaid dressed as a salmon!'

Meri swam over to him. 'Fortress Bay spy MP—'

'Stop right there,' Trevor said, flipping his tail up so it covered Meri's face. 'I know exactly who you are. It's Meri Pebble, isn't it?'

'You remember my real name?' Meri said.

'Of course,' Trevor said. 'We had How to Be Less Fortress Bay and More Normal classes together. Remember? I brushed my eyes with the toothbrush and failed?'

'An easy mistake to make,' Meri said, patting Trevor awkwardly on the arm. 'Great to see you.'

'I assume you're here on a top-secret mission and you need the exit for land,' Trevor said in a whisper. 'This way.'

He guided Steve and Meri to a queue and told them to buy tickets for a film called *Shellebration*.

Meri took her seat, placing Steve gently next to her.

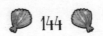

'What is it?' Trevor whispered, nodding at Steve.

'It's a talking seahorse stuck in a tube,' Meri said.

'And a miracle,' Steve whispered, trying to manoeuvre a sandbite through the tube with the very tip of his tail.

Meri wriggled with excitement. 'Where's the exit?'

'You'll have to watch some of the film first,' Trevor said. 'Sorry,' he added, before swimming off.

Meri and Steve spent the next ten minutes watching some shells with faces drawn on them having a party, which wasn't ideal, given they were in a hurry.

'If we find the exit ourselves, we could just swim through it,' Meri whispered to Steve, unable to bear any more *Shellebration*.

'But the big shellebration is about to begin – look how happy the shells are!' Steve said, now fully invested in the film.

Before Meri could reply, their chairs flipped around and disappeared under the floor!

The room beneath was a lot brighter and filled with

official-looking stacks of seaweed paper and mermaids typing away on large shell compacts.

Trevor appeared beside them dressed in his salmon costume. 'You'll just need to provide proof that you have permission to go to land and have been granted legs. Most mermaids have a form.'

'One moment,' Meri said, dragging Steve to the corner of the room.

'What is it?' Steve asked.

'I don't have a permission form,' Meri whispered.

'So what do we do?' Steve whispered back. 'We don't have much time!'

'We need to call your sister,' Meri explained. 'Sabrina's the only one who will grant me legs, but she's on holiday, so she won't answer my call. I'll just get diverted to the Teenies again.'

'You could send Sabrina an urgent message saying I'm in great danger,' Steve suggested. 'She'll be annoyed, but it will grab her attention.'

Meri punched some buttons on the clamshell compact and it began jiggling instantly.

'It's her!' Meri gasped.

'WHAT'S HAPPENED TO STEVE?' Sabrina said in a panic.

'I feel so loved,' Steve oozed.

'Um,' Meri said. 'He's all right. We actually wanted to speak to you about getting some legs.'

'WHY DID YOU SEND THAT MESSAGE IF HE'S ALL RIGHT? I'M ON HOLIDAY!'

'I *am* stuck in a tube,' Steve said, floating into view. 'If

that makes things better?'

'Why are you stuck in a tube?' Sabrina demanded.

'It's a long story involving half hamsters, half starfish,' Meri said.

They could hear Sabrina take a big gulp of a drink.

'Are you at the Leech Spa in Pinkly Lagoon?' Steve asked, sounding more than a little jealous. 'Are you drinking Gloopy?'

'No time for that now,' Meri said. 'We need legs for the mission.'

'What?' Sabrina choked. 'There's truth to that crabagram?'

'There is,' Meri said. 'But we've got it all under control.'

'Then why are you going to land?' Sabrina asked.

'Small complication,' Meri said. 'So small.'

'The Sushi Sisters got legs,' Steve blurted out. 'So Meri needs some too.'

'WHAT?' Sabrina roared. 'How did they get legs? I don't see any permissions on my clam compact.'

'It's a *mystery*,' Meri lied.

 148

'So they just *miraculously* got hold of some legs?' Sabrina said with suspicion in her voice.

'Um … we're still working that out.' Meri crossed her fingers behind her back. Beattie really owed her one now.

Sabrina sighed. 'I'D LIKE TO ORDER THREE MORE GLOOPYS PLEASE!'

'Sabrina?' Meri pressed. 'The legs?'

'I will send through a permission slip for legs immediately, and a large fishbowl for Steve,' Sabrina said. 'I expect this whole debacle to be wrapped up and back in the sea by tomorrow.'

'Yes, Sabrina,' Meri said.

Sabrina signed off. Within seconds a permission slip came shooting out of the oversized shell compact next to Trevor.

'Permission granted,' he said, pushing the rusted old door open. The water in the room didn't escape, but beyond Meri could see a human street.

Her tail tingled as it stretched and swivelled and morphed into legs, then she was spat out on to the pavement.

She looked down to see a tutu and some gold trainers.

'Seriously?' Meri said, staring at the bright pink puffy skirt that was not her style at all.

'The outfit is completely random,' Trevor said, floating on the other side of the door, 'unless you bring your own human clothes or request something specific. Once a spy got an inflatable pumpkin costume – and it wasn't even Halloween! Very difficult to blend in while wearing that one.'

Meri stumbled backwards and looked up at the door she'd come from.

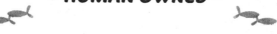

TREVOR TROUT'S
CHIPS AND FISH SHOP
– HUMAN OWNED –

'*Human owned*, how subtle,' Steve said from his new fishbowl. 'Also, it's definitely fish and chips, not chips and fish.'

But Meri wasn't listening, she had climbed a lamp post and was apparently looking for the Sushi Sisters.

'Excuse you!' Steve shouted. 'I don't see any other humans climbing lamp posts in tutus! I thought you wanted to blend in?'

'You're right,' Meri said, as she dropped down next to him and flipped open her clamshell compact.

'First we get backup from some other spy mermaids.'

'And where do we get that?' Steve asked.

'That's what I was looking for when I was up the lamp post.' Meri pointed across the road to a sign that said *SWIMMING POOL*.

24

Beattie's Big Mistake

As soon as they hit land, Beattie felt more like the Sushi Sisters' prisoner than their new best friend.

They had found a hotel near where the final prank would take place. But for now they were curled up in their room, drinking tea and eating biscuits and staring at their new kneecaps.

'I'm so glad you magically made us some legs,' Nolla laughed. 'We would have had to convince Meri to get us legs, but we knew you'd be so much easier to persuade, Beattie.'

Beattie smiled meekly. She'd begun to wonder if the Sushi Sisters were just using her, but they were still being quite nice to her, even now that they had exactly what they wanted.

'I *love* having legs, and I *love* your spotted skirt,'

Nolla said to Beattie.

It was the skirt Beattie had worn when she did her summer on land with legs. The Sushi Sisters had both changed into matching sushi-print leggings from Figgy Bass, with sparkly tartan trim and rips at the knees.

'What exactly *is* the final prank?' Beattie asked, but the Sushi Sisters didn't answer.

'I'm too excited to sleep,' Vetty said. 'We're going to be so famous after this!' She tapped the little goldfish-bowl shoulders on her top where the hamstars were being kept. 'The hamstars haven't been home in a while.'

'The hamstars came from land?' Beattie asked.

'Oh yes,' Nolla said. 'We did our summer on land with legs in this town, and we got the hamstars while we were here.'

'But hamstars are a mermaid thing,' Beattie said.

'Yes,' Nolla said with a smile. 'And we got them from a mermaid – he lives nearby in a loch.'

'We were so badly behaved that summer, Arabella Cod said she'd never give us legs again,' Vetty said, stretching hers over Beattie. 'She'll be furious when she finds out you magically gave them to us.'

'But you said it was for the prank,' Beattie said.

'It *is*,' Vetty said with a smirk.

'But I didn't realise you weren't *allowed* legs. You said it would be fine if I magically gave you legs – you said you had permission from Arabella Cod but you'd lost the slip!'

'Did we?' Vetty laughed.

'You're going to be in so much trouble with Arabella

Cod,' Nolla said, playfully pushing Beattie.

Beattie jumped to her feet, feeling her old, sensible self flooding back. 'We've got to return home. If we're not allowed to be here, then we shouldn't be.'

'It's too late,' Vetty said, shoving a biscuit in her mouth. 'You never know, Arabella Cod might love the prank and then all will be forgiven.'

'WHAT IS THE PRANK?' Beattie cried.

'You'll see,' the Sushi Sisters said together – 'SUSH!'

Beattie grimaced and thought of Zelda far away in the Hidden Lagoon. She'd been right all along – the Sushi Sisters were trouble.

She stared out of the window at a castle in the distance.

Little did she know, Zelda was right there.

25

The Pool Palace

Meri was an expert spy, so she managed to cross the road with only a few strange glances, and one shout of, 'WHAT IS THAT STRANGE GIRL WITH THE FISHBOWL DOING OUT AT THIS TIME OF NIGHT?'

As it *was* night-time, the swimming pool was empty. And it was also closed.

'How do we get in?' Meri said, rattling the huge padlock and chain wrapped around the door handles.

Steve manoeuvred himself in the fishbowl and inched his tail out of the tube. 'Put me near the lock, I'll pick it.'

It took just a matter of seconds to get in. Inside, huge waterslides towered over them and abandoned armbands littered the tiles.

 157

Meri dived into the pool, taking Steve with her. Her legs morphed into a tail as she swam towards the deep end, running her hand along the edge as she went.

'What exactly are you looking for?' Steve asked, just as Meri came to a stop next to a strange grate.

'This,' she said, pulling it off.

'Oh wow,' Steve whispered. 'There's a tunnel behind here.'

They followed the tunnel down into a secret pool filled with mermaid spies.

'Hello, hello, who have we got here then?' a mermaid with spiky black hair asked. She had the same spy tail as Meri and wore a black waistcoat.

'I'm Meri Pebble, spy MP 241, and you're Joey Sharkton,' Meri said, practically sinking in shock. 'The best land spy mermaid in the world.'

All around them spies were dancing, lounging on inflatable unicorns and drinking foam shakes under swimming-goggle decorations. Along the edges mermaids swam in and out of grates, greeting each other as they passed.

'We call this the POOL PALACE,' Joey Sharkton explained. 'It's our hang-out here on land.'

'Why do you all meet behind a grate in a public swimming pool in a tiny town in Scotland?' Steve asked.

Joey Sharkton threw her hands in the air. 'There is no place less likely for spy mermaids to be. We have a network of grates and tunnels that connect this swimming pool to others around the country, and even around the world.'

'Don't humans get suspicious of the strange grates?' Meri asked.

'Never,' Joey Sharkton said. 'Sometimes a child suggests something might be behind it – often a shark, which is funny, given my second name. But only spies with clam compacts can remove the grate to get inside.'

Meri flopped down on an inflatable doughnut next to a freshly poured foam shake.

'MERI,' Steve said, in a voice so high-pitched he made himself wince. 'SORRY, I DON'T KNOW WHAT'S HAPPENED TO MY VOICE. I THINK IT MIGHT BE THE CHLORINE.'

'We need help,' Meri said to Joey Sharkton. 'There are two mermaids on land right now who play pranks.'

'Oh, the Sushi Sisters!' Joey Sharkton cheered, making the other spy mermaids stop and stare. 'We LOVE their show!'

'No, no,' Meri said. 'They're up to something terrible. For their final prank, they're going to destroy all the humans!'

Joey Sharkton raised an eyebrow. 'That would be unusual.'

'Trust me,' Meri said, sipping her foam shake. 'I'm definitely right. I've seen the crabagram, and the shoes. I can't be wrong on this one.'

'We'll tail them and help you stop them before they do anything terrible,' Joey Sharkton said. 'You don't need to worry about a thing, we have your back.'

'SERIOUSLY, MERI, DO YOU THINK IT'S THE CHLORINE?' Steve squeaked. 'THIS MIGHT ACTUALLY HELP MY SINGING VOICE – I CAAAN REEEEACH SOME REEEALLY HIIIIGH NOTES NOW.'

161

'Come on, Steve,' Meri said. 'We need to find Zelda and Mimi, and I think I know just where to look.' She turned to Joey Sharkton. 'Could you point me in the direction of Paris Silkensocks's castle?'

26

Zelda Approves of Charks

The Flubiére party was in full swing, but Paris was desperate for Zelda and Mimi to meet her new friend Coral. And Zelda and Mimi were desperate to see the vanishing mermaid city of Corloch, complete with crabbits, which Paris had promised them she wasn't making up.

'We have to be quiet,' Paris said. 'And not do anything to attract attention.'

But the novelty of legs was too much for Zelda and she cartwheeled all the way down to the water's edge while Paris and Mimi darted from tree to tree.

The final cartwheel catapulted Zelda into the loch and her legs turned into a shimmering green tail.

'WAIT FOR ME!' Mimi squealed, belly-flopping in after her.

Paris shook her necklace and dived in, hoping no one at the party had seen them from a window.

Coral was waiting for them with a big grin on his face.

'You found your friends!' he cheered. 'Was it because I fixed your clam compact?'

'Not exactly,' Paris said, 'but thank you for doing that. This is Zelda and Mimi, my friends from the Hidden Lagoon.'

'Wow,' Coral said, bowing slightly. 'Hidden Lagoon mermaids!'

'And this is Coral,' Paris said. 'It's Mermaid for Carl.'

'Yes, I know that,' Zelda said, as something familiar and furry swam past. 'Wait, do you have hamstars here?'

'I do!' Coral said, beaming. 'I invented them myself. Zelda … can I ask you a question?'

'Of course,' Zelda said.

Coral glanced at Paris, who was shaking her head disapprovingly. 'How would you feel if I invented a CHARK?'

'Is that a … half chicken, half shark?' Zelda guessed.

 164

'It is!'

'THAT'S THE BEST THING I'VE EVER HEARD!' Zelda cheered.

'Oh good,' Coral said proudly. 'I invent all kinds of creatures. Humans even know about my mercats now, and they think they're adorable! Of course, they have no idea they're actually real!'

A mercat floated up and sat on Zelda's head.

'Do you know the Sushi Sisters?' she asked.

Coral looked surprised to hear the name.

'Nolla and Vetty? Yes, they came to Scotland for their summer on land with legs, but they spent most of it in this loch. They stole two hamstars.'

'Well, you might see them again soon,' Zelda said. 'They planned to get legs and come to Scotland – they want to destroy all the humans.'

'Destroy all the humans?' Coral cried. 'That's awful!'

'Wait a second,' Zelda said. 'They know this loch well – what if the reason they chose Scotland was because there was something here that they needed? I think this loch is the key to figuring out their plan—'

Before she could say any more, a shoal of pufferfish tore past her, knocking her sideways.

'WHAT IS GOING ON?' Coral shouted over to Paris, who was now caught in a pufferfish tornado.

'It's the pufferfish display for the party,' Paris groaned, as the fish accidentally scooped her up and broke through the surface.

Paris was catapulted into the air as pufferfish leapt up around her.

'It really is a bit like fireworks with fish,' Paris heard a partygoer musing.

She covered her face, hoping no one would notice the mermaid among the pufferfish.

'Is that a—?'

Paris grabbed her necklace and morphed into a jellyfish.

'But I saw a mermaid!' the person in the crowd said as Paris tumbled back underwater.

'She's a jellyfish!' Coral exclaimed, completely delighted. 'That necklace really is the best invention ever.'

'Yeah,' Zelda said, as Paris morphed back into a mermaid. 'It's pretty cool.'

'If you think the Sushi Sisters are coming here, then we should be on lookout so we can ambush them,' Paris said. 'Come on, I know a spot.'

27

The Whale Bus Arrives

'I can't be seeing that, can I?' Zelda said, peering out from the tree she and Paris were hiding in as they waited for the Sushi Sisters. Mimi was in a bush below, practising fin-fu moves on some sticks.

Paris was a good five feet below Zelda, as she hadn't wanted to climb up so high.

'I can't hear you, Zelda,' Paris whispered.

'Come up higher then!'

'I don't want to, I might fall.'

'But the whole point of legs is to break your fall, isn't it?' Zelda said.

'No, they just break,' Paris said wearily, as Zelda climbed down to where she was perched.

'I think I saw Jelly,' Zelda said, just as a whale came up for air in the loch, sporting a bus on its back.

'HELLO!' Jelly cried. 'WHALE BUS AHOY!'

'Knew it!' Zelda said.

'Oh my COD!' Paris cried. 'The Flubiérarty is still going on. No one must see her! How do we get her out of there?'

'The Flubiérwhatta?' said Zelda.

Jelly leaned out of the bus window. 'PARIS, I MANAGED TO GET THE WHALE BUS CLOSER TO YOU. DO YOU STILL WANT A RIDE BACK TO THE HIDDEN LAGOON?'

'How can she see me in this tree?' Paris whispered to Zelda.

'YOU THINK JUST

 170

BECAUSE I'M OLD I HAVE BAD HEARING AND BAD EYESIGHT? MY HEARING AND EYESIGHT GET BETTER AND BETTER – I PRACTICALLY HAVE X-RAY EYES!'

Paris leapt down from the tree and splashed through the water, climbing up the whale's nose to reach the bus. 'I'm actually going to stay here – turns out my mermaid friends came to me.'

Zelda waved from the tree.

'Oh well, that's wonderful,' Jelly said. 'Remember, if you need me, just call!' And with that she disappeared under the water.

A slightly frazzled Coral was floating just below the surface. He had about ten mercats attached to his face. 'Any more friends you want to bring here?' he asked Paris. 'The mercats aren't used to so many visitors … or whales with buses on them.'

'Sorry about that,' Paris said. 'I'm not expecting any more visitors.'

'PARIS!' came a cry, as Meri wandered up the drive in a tutu, cradling a fishbowl.

 171

Paris turned guiltily to Coral. 'OK, just one more friend.'

'STEVE'S STUCK IN A TUBE!' Meri called over, trying to explain the fishbowl.

'OK, two,' Paris said to Coral. 'Just two more friends.'

28

Sushmaid

It was sunrise by the time the guests left the Flubiérarty and the Sushi Sisters arrived, just as Zelda had predicted.

'I thought we were going to stick out among the humans with our orange lipstick and rainbow eyeshadow, but look,' Nolla said, as they strolled past the party guests, who were caked in Flubiére. 'Everyone here wears it!'

Beattie walked between them. She was already penning the sorry letter to Arabella Cod in her head. Trust her first ever rebellion to turn into an actual crime against the mermaid queen.

'You've got your legs,' Beattie said, 'so I might just leave.'

'Oh no,' Vetty said, pulling her close, as if she were

afraid of her running off. 'We need you for this next bit.'

'I might go and stay with a friend,' Beattie went on, hoping they would just let her go. 'I have a friend who lives in Scotland.'

'So do we,' the Sushi Sisters said. 'And for the final prank, you are going to meet him.'

They skipped down to the loch, dragging Beattie with them. Luckily Susan Silkensocks was fast asleep on top of some leftover carrots and didn't see them.

Beattie looked around the eerily still loch, drenched in shadows from the nearby trees. What would they find beneath the water?

They dived under, their tails reappearing as they did.

Beattie was surprised to see there was nothing down there, just rocks and seaweed and the occasional eel.

They swam deeper, skimming the floor of the loch with their stomachs.

'Oh Coral!' the Sushi Sisters cried. 'Come out, come out, wherever you are!'

Beattie felt something pull at her tail. She whipped round, but there was nothing there.

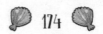 174

'I waaaaassss rrreeeaaallyyy mmmeeeeeeaaaaannnn toooooooooo mmmmyyyyyy frrrrriiiieeeeennnndddd Zeeeeeeellllllddddaaaa,' came a ghostly voice.

'Did you hear that?' Beattie hissed, ducking behind some seaweed. 'It sounded like a ghost!'

The Sushi Sisters burst out laughing, just as a face began to appear.

Beattie screamed!

'What?' Nolla said, pointing at the mermaid boy. 'It's only Coral! He's our friend.'

Coral looked at Beattie and flashed her a kind smile. She was sure he nodded at the rocks next to him, as if trying to draw her attention to them.

'Coral, we're here to film the final episode of our TV show,' Vetty said, whipping out a camera. 'We'll need your inventing lab.'

'What for?' came a familiar growl.

Beattie stared in astonishment as her friends – Paris, Meri, Zelda, Mimi and Steve – emerged from the rocks as if by magic.

'You can disguise yourself very easily in this loch. It's

 175

something to do with octopus intelligence,' Mimi chirped.

'You're here,' Beattie said, her voice wobbling. She was so happy to see them she thought she might cry.

'Yes, but *why* are you all here?' the Sushi Sisters said. 'SUSH!'

'STOP SAYING SUSH!' Steve cried, in his high-pitched voice. Then, 'SORRY, I'VE BEEN IN A SWIMMING POOL AND IT'S TEMPORARILY ALTERED MY VOICE.'

'And you're still stuck in a tube,' Beattie said, wishing she could swim over and help him, but the Sushi Sisters held her back.

'We're not alone,' Meri said, as an entire army of spy mermaids appeared behind her – hundreds and hundreds of them, led by Joey Sharkton. 'You will not destroy the humans!'

Nolla and Vetty burst out laughing. 'So you got our crabagram?'

'I knew you sent it,' Meri said. 'You realised Arabella Cod wasn't going to give you legs, so you thought you'd try to get a spy. For that, you needed to reveal your evil plan in a crabagram and have a spy find it in the crabagram network. You would then befriend the spy – me! – in the hope that I would give you legs. And, failing that, you would steal my clam compact and request them yourself.'

Vetty smiled. 'Very good.'

'But then you discovered Beattie's secret – you saw her do magic, and you realised you had found something rarer than a spy – you had found a water witch.'

'Yeah, thanks for bringing her,' Nolla said.

'You then made Beattie feel like the favourite, you even said she could be a Sushi Sister. You convinced her to magic you up some legs, and then you came here to put your plan into action. You came here to destroy all the humans!'

Nolla was nodding until the last bit. 'Wait, NO!'

'No, what?' Meri said.

'The destroying the humans bit was just made up for the crabagram to get your attention. We're not going to do anything to the humans, we're only

interested in our final prank.'

'We're going to make a Sushmaid!' the Sushi Sisters cheered together. 'Sush!'

'A *WHAT*?' Beattie, Mimi, Zelda, Paris and Meri cried.

'Uh-oh,' Coral said quietly. 'It might be worse than a chark …'

'A Sushmaid,' Nolla said, as if it should be obvious, 'is a half sushi, half mermaid. We came here to use Coral's laboratory, because we're going to make Beattie into one! And we are going to present the episode with legs and surprise everyone! It will be the greatest prank of all time! And also very in keeping with our rebellious style.'

'I thought you were trying to destroy the humans or take over the world,' Meri said.

'Ew,' Nolla said. 'If we take over the world then we would be *responsible* for *the world*. The only thing I want to be responsible for is me, my hair and my hamstar.'

'Oh well, that's a relief!' Zelda said.

'A relief?' Beattie cried. 'Zelda, they're going to

make me HALF SUSHI!'

'It's just such a relief after meeting so many mermaids who want world domination,' Zelda said.

'I …' Meri began, staring at the huge spy army she had called in. 'I … have possibly overreacted slightly. I'm sorry … I don't know what got into me! I think I was so desperate for a dangerous mission that I saw what I wanted to see. I still have a lot to learn …'

Joey Sharkton patted her on the back. 'Happens to the best of us,' she said. 'Right, gang, back to the Pool Palace!'

Meri watched as one by one the spies leapt out of the loch.

'I'm so relieved,' Zelda said, putting her arm around Meri.

'HELLO?' Beattie cried to her friends. 'There's still a small problem involving me being made into a half sushi!'

'It's a Sushmaid,' Nolla said.

Vetty nodded. 'Or a Merushi.'

'You're not actually going to let them do it, are you?'

Beattie said. 'Please don't let them!'

'You have been kind of annoying,' Zelda said. 'And mean.'

'I know!' Beattie said. 'And I'm sorry! I shouldn't have tried to be cool like the Sushi Sisters. I wanted to stop being the one who worries all the time, but instead I stopped caring about anyone and I was hurtful. I should've shared my worries with you and then they would be smaller and easier to handle.'

'And I should've been more thoughtful,' Zelda said. 'It's easy to be carefree and reckless when I have a friend who will fix everything for me, but I need to be responsible too. That's why I got legs and flew all the way here. Because that's what you would've done.'

'We're still turning her into a Sushmaid or Merushi,' the Sushi Sisters said firmly. 'We've worked really hard to set all this up. Just imagine – our last prank of the series is to make a mermaid into our FAVOURITE THING.'

'You weren't lying about them,' Paris said, staring at the Sushi Sisters in amazement. 'They are very strange.'

'Who is this?' the Sushi Sisters asked.

Zelda grinned. 'She's Paris, and if you trust me and my creative vision, she's going to give you the greatest prank for your TV show you could possibly imagine. A prank even better than turning Beattie into a Sushmaid.'

The Tartan Times

Everyone is convinced Gail McBagpipes has been hit on the head, because she's claiming she saw some very strange things pop out of the loch during Susan Silkensocks's party.

Shoals of pufferfish created a fireworks-but-with-fish display, and everyone in the town loved it. But Gail McBagpipes insists she saw a mermaid that morphed into a jellyfish MID-AIR, and a disgruntled mercat.

Gail McBagpipes is known for spotting strange things. She's seen Nessie four thousand times, a ghost mermaid a handful of times, a mermaid who morphs into a jellyfish once, and her latest claim, just in, is that she saw an old lady driving a bus on the back of a whale.

29

Sleepover in the Hidden Lagoon!

Back in the Hidden Lagoon, Beattie was not a Sushmaid, or a Merushi. She was just Beattie, having another sleepover with her best friends Mimi and Zelda.

'THE HIDDEN LAGOON IS AMAZING!' Coral squealed as he swam in through the window with a *Clippee* T-shirt and glasses, a stack of chomp chops from Jawella's, a foam shake from the Crab Café and a pile of Sandbury's shopping bags.

'I've given him a tour of all the good spots,' Paris said, nestling down on the bed next to Beattie's brand-new hamstar. 'What have you called it?' she asked.

Beattie smiled. 'Sushmaid.'

'Well, little Sushmaid,' Paris said, tickling its starfish belly. 'I will see you very soon.'

'Oh, are you leaving already?' Meri said, as she swam through the window.

'I've got to catch the whale bus back – Jelly isn't making another trip to Salmon City for a week, so I can't miss this one. Could you imagine if I was gone for a whole week? My mother would definitely figure out what I was up to!'

'We'll miss you!' Zelda called over. Her eyes were glued to a shockey match on TV. Her other best friend Rachel Rocker was playing.

'BAD FISH!' she shouted, as an octopus hurled a player across the track. 'I can't wait to get back on the team and win the next match.'

'Thanks so much for having me in the lagoon,' Coral said. 'I'll come back with Paris soon. Maybe we'll invent a quick way of getting here.'

'Oh, you'd better come back soon,' Zelda said. 'You're in our gang now, Coral.'

'I am?' he said. 'Oh wow, I'm so happy. I've never had friends and now I have loads!'

'Don't be too happy about it,' Zelda said. 'Normally,

 185

we have to save the world. Consider the Sushi Sisters your training.'

He nodded obediently, and he and Paris set off towards the whale bus, waving and blowing huge bubble kisses to the others as they went.

'Hey,' a mermaid said, stopping Paris. 'You look just like the human from the Sushi Sisters' latest prank.'

Paris just laughed. 'Right, Coral,' she said. 'Time to go home.'

Beattie and the others waved from the window until they were out of sight, and then returned to their foam shakes.

'What should we do?' Mimi asked.

'We could watch a really bad film,' Meri suggested. 'It's called *Shellebration*.'

'Oh!' Beattie said. 'The one about the shells having a party!'

Mimi looked enthused. 'That sounds WONDERFUL. Let's definitely watch it.'

Beattie flopped on to the seaweed rug and smiled.

 186

'I'm so lucky to have such good friends,' she whispered.

Steve came charging into the room, still stuck in his tube. 'AND A MIRACLE SEAHORSE!' he screeched in her ear.

'And a miracle seahorse,' Beattie said with a big smile.

CLAMZINE

THE *SUSHI SISTERS' PRANKATHON* WOWS WITH A FABULOUS HUMAN PRANK!

It's been nothing but rave reviews for the Sushi Sisters' final prank, which saw them hand a mercat to a human and watch the reaction.

The human, a young girl in excellent socks called Paris, squealed with excitement when she realised the mercat was half fish – and she fell into a loch!

Although the prank has been criticised by some for being too risky, given it took place in the human world, the Sushi Sisters were very clever to pick a town where there have been so many strange sightings over the years, no human was likely to believe it.

Mermaids have delighted in getting a look at a real human, and many fans have had fun debating how the Sushi Sisters got legs.

The episode is the Sushi

Sisters' most popular to date.

When speaking to *Clamzine*, the famous mermaids said they were inspired by some friends who made them realise pranks don't need to be mean.

They said they also plan to return Wigbert Krill's moustache, and they let the human girl keep the mercat.

She has named him Gadgets.

BAD Mermaids

Read the whole fabulously fishy series!

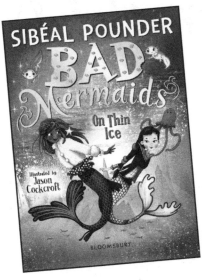

AVAILABLE NOW!

There is a world where
witches live, deep down
below the sink pipes ...

Read on for a sneak peek at the
first book in Sibéal Pounder's
Witch Wars series

AVAILABLE NOW!

THE COVES

SINKVILLE

PEARL PEAK

PEARL PEAK ACADEMY

FOREST

LITTLE LEAF RESTAURANT

WHERE THE FIRST WITCH LANDED IN SINKVILLE

BROLLYWOOD

FAIRY CARAVAN PARK

THE CAULDRON ISLANDS

BUBBLE BEACH

THE OLD CAULDRON FACTORY

197

THE TOWERS

Prologue

For as long as anyone can remember, witches have lurked on this planet. They have brewed gloopy potions in their cauldrons and torn through the sky on their brooms. They have cackled. They have cursed. They have cats.

Most people think witches are really evil, with their tattered black dresses, pointy hats and unfortunate noses, but that's mostly nonsense and really only half the story. The truth, if you happen to be looking for it, lies deep down below the sink pipes ...

1

Down the Plughole

It would have been very difficult to spot Fran the fairy on the day this story begins. Her dress may have been puffy, her hair may have been huge, but she was barely the size of a small potato.

Fran was slowly sidestepping across a garden lawn, holding a large, limp leaf in front of her. She didn't want the owner of the garden to see her because Miss Heks was a terrible old woman with a grim face and size eleven shoes. If she had seen Fran she would've squashed her immediately.

Fran and her leaf were on a mission. There was something very important in the shed at the bottom of Miss Heks's garden. That something was a girl called Tiga Whicabim.

3

'You!' Tiga said, pointing at a slug that was sliding its way across an old stone sink. 'You will be the star of my show! You will play the role of Beryl, an ambitious dancer with severe hiccups.'

Tiga had been in the shed for hours. The evil Miss Heks had been her guardian for as long as Tiga could remember and she had quickly learned to keep out of her way. If she didn't, the old bat would make her sew up the holes in her disgusting, scratchy dresses. Or she would force Tiga to run up and down the garden in her gigantic, ugly shoes, bellowing things like 'FASTER!' and 'OH, DID YOU TRIP?' from the kitchen window.

Tiga shone a torch on the slug.

'You are going to be the best actor the world has ever seen!' she cried.

Fran sighed when she saw that.

Not because she'd finally found Tiga, after a long and perilous journey that had almost ended with her being eaten by a dog.

 4

No, the reason Fran sighed was because she loved a bit of acting!

Despite her small size, Fran was a big deal in the world of show business. Everyone called her Fran the Fabulous Fairy (a name she had made up for herself). She had hosted many award-winning TV shows like *Cooking for Tiny People* and *The Squashed and the Swatted* and she'd played the lead role in *Glittery Sue* – a tragic drama about a small lady called Sue who got some glitter in her hair and couldn't get it out again.

'An actor you say!' Fran said, making Tiga jump.

Tiga stared, mouth open, at the small person that marched across the shed and – very ungracefully, and with much grunting – climbed up the leg of her trusty old rocking chair.

Fran stretched out a hand.

'Very delighted to meet you, Tiga! Now, it's pronounced *Teega*, isn't it? That's what I thought! I'm very good at names and absolutely everything else. I'm Fran the Fabulous Fairy. But you can call me Fran. Or Fabulous. BUT NEVER JUST FAIRY. I hate that.'

Tiga, understandably, assumed she had gone mad. Or at the very least fallen asleep.

She squinted at the little thing with big hair and then looked to the slug for reassurance, but it was sliding its way across the floor as if it knew exactly who Fran was, and was trying to escape.

'I don't think,' Fran said, pointing at the slug, 'that she should be acting in the lead role. She is slimy and not paying much attention.'

Fran wiggled a foot and a beehive of hair just like her own appeared on top of the slug's head.

'Much, much, *much* better,' she said.

Tiga panicked – the slug had *hair*! Not any old hair, a beehive of perfectly groomed hair! It was a split-second reaction, but with a flick of her hand she batted the fairy clean off the rocking chair.

Fran wobbled from left to right and tried to steady herself.

'Did you just *swat* me?' she snapped. 'The ultimate insult!'

Tiga tried to avoid eye contact and instead looked at

the slug. She couldn't be sure, but it looked a lot like it was shaking its head at her.

'WITCHES ARE NOT ALLOWED TO SWAT FAIRIES. IT IS THE LAW,' Fran ranted.

'I'm sorry!' Tiga cried. 'I didn't think you were real – I thought you were just my imagination! You don't need to call me a witch.'

'Yes I do,' said Fran, floating in front of Tiga with her hands on her hips. 'Because you are one.'

'I am one what?' Tiga asked.

'One witch,' said Fran as she twirled in the air, got her puffy dress caught in her wings and crash-landed on the floor.

'BRAAAAT!' came a bellow from across the garden. 'Time to leave the shed. Your dinner is ready!'

Tiga glanced nervously out of the window. 'If you are real, although I'm still not convinced you are, you'd better leave now. Miss Heks is a terrible old woman and she will do horrible, nasty, ear-pinching things to you.'

Fran ignored her and went back to twirling in the air. 'What are you having for dinner?'

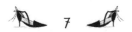

'Cheese water,' Tiga said with a sigh. 'It's only ever cheese water.'

Fran thought about this for a moment. 'And how do you make this cheese water?'

'You find a bit of mouldy old cheese and you put it in some boiling water,' said Tiga, looking ill.

Fran swooped down lower and landed on the sink. 'Well, I'm afraid we don't have cheese water in Ritzy City – it's mostly cakes.'

Tiga stared at the fairy. 'Ritzy where?'

'*Riiiitzzzzzy Ciiiiity!*' Fran cheered, waving her hands in the air.

Tiga shrugged. 'Never heard of it.'

'But you're a witch,' said Fran.

'I am not a witch!' Tiga cried.

'You SO are!'

'I am not!'

'Definitely are,' said Fran, nodding her head. 'Even your name says so.'

And with that she flicked her tiny finger, sending a burst of glittery dust sailing across the room.

8

TIGA WHICABIM, the dust read.

Then it began to wobble and rearrange itself into something new.

I AM A BIG WITCH.

'You've cheated somehow,' Tiga mumbled, moving the dust letters about in the air. Most people would've believed Fran by this point, but Tiga wasn't used to magic and fun and insane fairies. So, despite this very

convincing evidence that she might just be a witch, Tiga still walked towards the door. Towards the cheese water.

'TIGA!' bellowed Miss Heks. 'YOUR CHEESE WATER HAS REACHED BOILING POINT.'

'Cheese water,' Fran chuckled. 'Wait! Where are you going, Tiga?'

'To eat dinner,' said Tiga. 'Bye, Fabulous Fairy Fran. It was lovely to meet you.'

Fran raised a hand in the air. 'Wait! *What?* You're not coming with me to Ritzy City, a place of wonder and absolutely no cheese?'

Tiga paused. Even if it was a mad dream, it was better than cheese water. She turned on her heel and walked back towards Fran.

Fran squealed and squeaked and did somersaults in the air.

'WHAT'S GOING ON IN THERE? I KNOW YOU CAN HEAR ME, YOU LITTLE MAGGOT!' Miss Heks shouted.

Tiga could see Miss Heks stomping her way towards the shed.

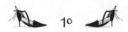

'Quick!' Fran cried. 'We must go to Ritzy City right now!'

'*How?*' Tiga cried, frantically looking around the shed for an escape route.

'Down the sink pipes, of course,' Fran said as she shot through the air and straight down the plughole.

'Come on, Tiga!' her shrill little voice echoed from somewhere inside the sink.

Tiga leaned over the stone sink and stared down the plughole.

There was nothing down there. No light. And certainly no city, that was for sure.

The door to the shed flew open and splinters of old wood went soaring through the air.

'WHAT IS GOING ON?' Miss Heks bellowed.

'NOW!' Fran yelled.

Tiga wiggled a finger in the plughole.

This is nonsense, she thought, just as she disappeared.

WITCH WARS

Read the whole ritzy,
glitzy, witchy series!

AVAILABLE NOW!